The Heart of Princess Osra

By Anthony Hope

"Kill him for me, then; kill him for me."

THE HEART OF
PRINCESS OSRA

BY

ANTHONY HOPE

WITH ILLUSTRATIONS
BY
H. C. EDWARDS

Originally published by
Frederick A. Stokes Company, 1896

Published by:
The Paper Tiger, Inc.
335 Jefferson Avenue
Cresskill, NJ 07626
(201) 567-5620
www.papertig.com

Book design by Mark Van Horne

ISBN: 1-889439-12-6 (PB)
ISBN: 1-889439-13-4 (HC)

CONTENTS

Chapter I

The Happiness of Stephen the Smith

"Stephen! Stephen! Stephen!"

The impatient cry was heard through all the narrow gloomy street, where the old richly-carved house-fronts bowed to meet one another and left for the eye's comfort only a bare glimpse of blue. It was, men said, the oldest street in Strelsau, even as the sign of the "Silver Ship" was the oldest sign known to exist in the city. For when Aaron Lazarus the Jew came there, seventy years before, he had been the tenth man in unbroken line that took up the business; and now Stephen Nados, his apprentice and successor, was the eleventh. Old Lazarus had made a great business of it, and had spent his savings in buying up the better part of the street; but since Jews then might hold no property in Strelsau, he had taken all the deeds in the name of Stephen Nados; and when he came to die, being unable to carry his houses or his money with him, having no kindred, and caring not a straw for any man or woman alive save Stephen, he bade Stephen let the deeds be, and, with a last curse against the Christians (of whom Stephen was one, and a devout one), he kissed the young man, and turned his face to the wall and died. Therefore Stephen was a rich man, and had no need to carry on the business, though it never entered his mind to do anything else; for half the people who raised their heads at the sound of the cry were Stephen's tenants, and paid him rent when he asked for it; a thing he did when he chanced to remember, and could tear himself away from chasing a goblet or fashioning a little silver saint; for Stephen loved his craft more than his rents; therefore, again, he was well liked in the quarter.

"Stephen! Stephen!" cried Prince Henry, impatiently hammering on the closed door with his whip." Plague take the man! Is he dead?"

The men in the quarter went on with their work; the women moved idly to the doors; the girls came out into the street and clustered here and there, looking at the Prince. For although he was not so handsome as that scamp Rudolf, his brother, who had just come back from his travels with half a dozen wild stories spurring after him, yet Henry was a comely youth, as he sat on his chestnut mare, with his blue eyes full of impatience, and his chestnut curls fringing his shoulders. So the girls clustered and looked. Moreover Stephen the smith must come soon, and the sight of him was worth a moment's waiting; for he buried himself all day in his workshop, and no laughing challenge could lure him out.

"Though, in truth," said one of the girls, tossing her head, "it's thankless work to spend a glance on either, for they do not return it. Now when Rudolf comes—"

She broke off with a laugh, and her comrades joined in it. Rudolf left no debts of that sort unpaid, however deep he might be in the books of Stephen Nados and of the others who furnished his daily needs.

Presently Stephen came, unbolting his door with much deliberation, and greeting Prince Henry with a restrained courtesy. He was not very well pleased to see his guest, for it was a ticklish moment with the nose of Saint Peter, and Stephen would have liked to finish the job uninterrupted. Still, the Prince was a prince, a gentleman, and a friend, and Stephen would not be uncivil to him.

"You ride early to-day, sir," he observed, patting the chestnut mare.

"I have a good reason," answered Henry. "The Lion rages to-day."

Stephen put up his hand to shelter his eyes from a ray of sunshine that had evaded the nodding walls and crept in; it lit up his flaxen hair, which he wore long and in thick waves, and played in his yellow beard and he looked very grave. For when the Lion raged, strange and alarming things might happen in the city of Strelsau. The stories of his last fit of passion were yet hardly old.

"What has vexed the King?" he asked; for he knew that Prince Henry spoke of his father, Henry surnamed the Lion, now an old man, yet as fierce as when he had been young. "Is it your brother again?"

"For a marvel, no. It is myself, Stephen. And he is more furious with me than he has ever been with Rudolf; aye, even more than he was at all the stories that followed my brother home."

"And what is the cause of it all, sir, and how is it in my power to help?"

"That you will find out very soon," said the Prince with a bitter laugh. "You will be sent for to the palace in an hour, Stephen."

"If it is about the King's ring, the ring is not finished," said Stephen.

"It is not about the ring. Yet indeed it is, in a way, about a ring. For you are to be married, Stephen. This very day you are to be married."

"I think not, sir," said Stephen mildly. "For it is a thing that a man himself hears about if it be true."

"But the King thinks so; Stephen, have you remarked, among my sister Osra's ladies, a certain dark lady, with black hair and eyes? I cannot describe her eyes."

"But you can tell me her name, sir," suggested Stephen, who was a practical man.

"Her name? Oh, her name is Hilda—Hilda von Lauengram."

"Aye, I know the Countess Hilda. I have made a bracelet for her."

"She is the most beautiful creature alive!" cried Prince Henry, in a sudden rapture and so loudly (being carried away by his passion) that the girls heard him and wondered of whom he spoke with so great an enthusiasm.

"To those to whom she seems such," observed Stephen. "But, pray, how am I concerned in all this, sir?"

The Prince's smile grew more bitter as he answered:

"Why, you are to marry her. It was an idle suggestion of Osra's, made in jest; my father is pleased to approve of it in earnest."

Then he bent in his saddle and went on in a hurried urgent whisper: "I love her better than my life, Stephen—better than heaven; and my faith and word are pledged to her; and last night I was to have fled with her—for I knew better than to face the old Lion—but Osra found her making preparations and we were discovered. Then Osra was scornful, and the King mad, and Rudolf laughed; and when they talked of what was to be done to her, Osra came in with her laughing suggestion. It caught the King's angry fancy, and he swore that it should be so. And, since the Archbishop is away, he has bidden the Bishop of Modenstein be at the palace at twelve to-day, and you will be brought there also, and you will be married to her. But, by heavens, I'll have your blood if you are!" With this sudden outbreak of fury the Prince ended. Yet a moment later, he put out his hand to the smith, saying: "It's not your fault, man."

"That's true enough," said the smith; "for I have no desire to marry her; and it is not fitting that a lady of her birth should mate with a smith; she is of a great house, and she would hate and despise me."

Prince Henry was about to assent when his eye chanced to fall on Stephen the smith. Now the smith was a very handsome man—handsomer, many said, than Prince Rudolf himself, whom no lady could look on without admiration; he stood six feet and two inches in his flat working shoes; he was very broad, and could leap higher and hurl a stone farther than any man in Strelsau. Moreover he looked kind and gentle, yet was reputed to grow angry at times, and then to be very dangerous. Therefore Prince Henry, knowing (or thinking that he knew) the caprices of women, and how they are caught by this and that, was suddenly seized with a terrible fear that the Countess Hilda might not despise Stephen the smith. Yet he did not express his fear, but said that it was an impossible thing that a lady of the Countess's birth (for the House of Lauengram was very noble) should wed a silversmith, even though he were as fine a fellow as his good friend Stephen; to which gracious speech Stephen made no reply, but stood very thoughtful, with his hand on the neck of the chestnut mare. But at last he said: "In any case it cannot be, for I am bound already."

"A wife? Have you a wife?" cried the Prince eagerly.

"No; but my heart is bound," said Stephen the smith.

"The King will make little of that. Yet who is she? Is she any of these girls who stand looking at us?"

"No, she is none of these," answered Stephen, smiling as though such an idea were very ludicrous.

"And are you pledged to her?"

"I to her, but not she to me."

"But does she love you?"

"I think it most unlikely," said Stephen the smith.

"The Lion will care nothing for this," groaned the Prince despondently. "They will send for you in half an hour. For heaven's sake spare her, Stephen!"

"Spare her, sir?"

"Do not consent to marry her, however urgently the King may command you."

The smith shook his head, smiling still. Prince Henry rode sorrowfully away, spending not a glance on the bevy of girls who watched him go; and Stephen, turning into his house, shut the door, and with one great sigh set to work again on the nose of Saint Peter.

"For anyhow," said he, "a man can work." And after a long pause he added, "I never thought to tell any one; but if I must, I must."

Now, sure enough, when the clock on the Cathedral wanted a quarter of an hour of noon, two of the King's Guard came and bade Stephen follow them with all haste to the palace; and since they were very urgent and no time was to be lost, he followed them as he was, in his apron, without washing his hands or getting rid of the dust that hung about him from his work. However he had finished Saint Peter's nose and all had gone well with it, so that he went in a contented frame of mind, determined to tell the whole truth to King Henry the Lion sooner than be forced into a marriage with the Countess Hilda von Lauengram.

The Lion sat in his great chair; he was a very thin old man, with a face haggard and deeply lined; his eyes, set far back in his head, glowed and glowered, and his fingers pulled his sparse white beard. On his right Prince Rudolf lolled on a low seat, smiling at the play; on his left sat that wonderfully fair lady, the Princess Osra, then in the first bloom of her young beauty; and she was smiling scornfully. Prince Henry stood before his father, and some yards from him was the Countess Hilda, trembling and tearful, supported by one of her companions; and finally, since the Archbishop was gone to Rome to get himself a Scarlet Hat, the Bishop of Modenstein, a young man of noble family, was there, most richly arrayed in choicest lace and handsomest vestments, ready to perform the ceremony. Prince Rudolf had beckoned the Bishop near him, and was jesting with him in an undertone. The Bishop laughed as a man laughs who knows he should not laugh but cannot well help himself; for Rudolf owned a pretty wit, although it was sadly unrestrained.

The King's fury, having had a night and a morning to grow cool in, had now settled into a cold ironical mood, which argued no less resolution than his first fierce wrath. There was a grim smile on his face as he addressed the smith, who, having bowed to the company, was standing between the Countess and Prince Henry.

"The House of Elphberg," said the King, with mocking graciousness, "well recognises your worth, Stephen, my friend. We are indebted to you—"

"It's a thousand crowns or more from Prince Rudolf alone, sire," interrupted Stephen, with a bow to the Prince he named.

"For much faithful service," pursued the King, while Rudolf laughed again. "I have therefore determined to reward you with the hand of a lady who is, it may be, above your station, but in no way above your worth. Behold her! Is she not handsome? On my word, I envy you, smith. She is beautiful, young, high-born. You are lucky, smith. Nay, no thanks. It is but what you deserve—and no more than she deserves. Take her and be happy," and he ended with a snarling laugh, as he waved his lean veined hand towards the unhappy Countess, and fixed his sneering eyes on the face of his son Henry, who had turned pale as death, but neither spoke nor moved.

The Bishop of Modenstein—he was of the House of Hentzau, many of which have been famous in history—lifted up his hands in horror at Rudolf's last whispered jest, and then, advancing with a bow to the King, asked if he were now to perform his sacred duties.

"Aye, get on with it," growled the Lion, not heeding the Countess's sobs or the entreaty in his son's face. And the Princess Osra sat unmoved, the scornful smile still on her lips; it seemed as though she had no pity for a brother who could stoop, or for a girl who had dared to soar too high.

"Wait, wait!" said Stephen the smith. "Does this lady love me, sire?"

"Aye, she loves you enough for the purpose, smith," grinned the King. "Do not be uneasy."

"May I ask her if she loves me, sire?"

"Why, no, smith. Your King's word must be enough for you."

"And your Majesty says that she loves me?"

"I do say so, smith."

"Then," said Stephen, "I am very sorry for her; for as there's a heaven above us, sire, I do not love her."

Prince Rudolf laughed; Osra's smile broadened in greater scorn; the Countess hid her face in her companion's bosom. The old King roared out a gruff burst. "Good, good!" he chuckled. "But it will come with marriage, smith; for with marriage love either comes or goes—eh, son Rudolf?—and since in this case it cannot go, you must not doubt, friend Stephen, that it will come." And he threw himself back in his chair, greatly amused that a smith, when offered the hand of a Countess, should hesitate to take it. He had not thought of so fine a humiliation as this for the presumptuous girl.

"That might well be, sire," admitted Stephen, "were it not that I most passionately love another."

"Take her and be happy."

"Our affections," said the King, "are unruly things, smith, and must be kept in subjection; is it not so, son Rudolf?"

"It should be so, sire," answered the merry Prince.

But the Princess Osra, whose eyes had been scanning Stephen's figure, here broke suddenly into the conversation.

"Are you pledged to her whom you love so passionately?" she asked.

"I have not ventured to tell her of my love, madame," answered he, bowing low.

"Then there is no harm done," observed Prince Rudolf. "The harm lies in the telling, not in the loving."

"Tell us something about her," commanded the Princess; and the King, who loved sport most when it hurt others, chimed in: "Aye, let's hear about her whom you prefer to this lady. In what shop does she work, smith? Or does she sell flowers? Or is she a serving-girl? Come, listen, Countess, and hear about your rival."

Prince Henry took one step forward in uncontrolled anger; but he could not meet the savage mirth in the old man's eyes, and, sinking into a chair, spread his hand across his face. But Stephen, regarding the King with placid good-humour, began to speak of her whom be loved so passionately. And his voice was soft as he spoke.

"She works in no shop, sire," said he, "nor does she sell flowers, nor is she a serving-girl; though I would not care if she were. But one day, when the clouds hung dark over our street, she came riding down it, and another girl with her. The two stopped before my door, and, see-ing them, I came out—"

"It is more than you do for me," remarked Prince Rudolf.

Stephen smiled, but continued his story. "I came out; and she whom I love gave me a bracelet to mend. And I, looking at her rather than at the bracelet, said, 'But already it is perfect.' But she did not hear, for, when she had given me the bracelet, she rode on again at once and took no more notice of me than of the flies that were crawling up my wall. That was the first and is the last time that I have spoken to her until this day. But she was so beautiful that there and then I swore that, until I had found means and courage to tell her my love, and until she had thrice refused it, I would marry no other maiden nor speak a word of love."

"It seems to me," said Prince Rudolf, "that the oath has some pru-dence in it; for if she prove obdurate, friend Stephen, you will then be able to go elsewhere; many lovers swear more intemperately."

"But they do not keep their oaths," said Stephen, with a shrewd look at the Prince.

"You had best let him alone, my son," said the old King. "He knows what all the country knows of its future King."

"Then he may go and hang with all the country," said the Prince peevishly.

But the Princess Osra leant a little forward towards Stephen, and the Countess Hilda also looked covertly out from the folds of her friend's dress at Stephen. And the Princess said:

"Was she then so beautiful, this girl?"

"As the sun in heaven, madame," said the smith.

"As beautiful as my pretty sister?" asked Rudolf in careless jest.

"Yes, as beautiful, sir," answered Stephen.

"Then," said the cruel old King, "very much more beautiful than this Countess?"

"Of that you must ask your son Henry, sire," said Stephen discreetly.

"Nevertheless," said the King, "you must put up with the Countess. We cannot all have what we want in this world, can we, son Henry?" and he chuckled again most maliciously.

"Not, sire, till my lady has thrice refused me," the smith reminded the King.

"Then she must be quick about it. For we all, and my lord Bishop here, are waiting. Send for her, Stephen—by heaven, I have a curiosity to see her!"

"And, by heaven! so have I," added Prince Rudolf with a merry smile. "And poor Henry here may be cured by the sight."

The Princess Osra leant a little further forward, and said gently:

"Tell us her name, and we will send for her. Indeed I also would like to see her."

"But if she refuses, I shall be worse off than I am now; and if she says yes, still I must marry the Countess," objected the smith.

"Nay," said the King, "if she does not refuse you three times, you shall not marry the Countess, but shall be free to try your fortune with the girl;" for the smith had put the Lion in a better temper, and he thought he was to witness more sport.

"Since your Majesty is so good, I must tell her name," said Stephen, "though I had rather have declared my love to herself alone."

"It is the pleasantest way," said Prince Rudolf, "but the thing can be done in the presence of others also."

"You must tell us her name that we may send for her," said the Princess, her eyes wandering now from the Countess to the smith, and back to the Countess again.

"Well, then," said Stephen sturdily, "the lady who came riding down the street and took away my heart with her is called Osra, and her father is named Henry."

A moment or two passed before they understood what the smith had said. Then the old King fell into a fit of laughter, half choked by coughing; Prince Rudolf clapped his hands in merry mockery, and a deep flush spread over the face of the Princess; while the Countess, her companion, and the younger Prince seemed too astonished to do anything but stare. As for Stephen, having said what he had to say, he held his peace—a thing in him which many men, and women also, would do well to imitate; and, if they cannot, let them pray for the grace that is needful. Heaven is omnipotent.

The old King, having recovered from his fit of laughing, looked round on the smith with infinite amusement, and, turning to his daughter, he said: "Come, Osra, you have heard the declaration. It remains only for you to satisfy our good friend's conscience by refusing him three times. For then he will be free to do our pleasure and make the Countess Hilda happy."

The heart of women is, as it would seem, a strange thing; for the Princess Osra, hearing what the smith had said and learning that he had fallen passionately in love with her on the mere sight of her beauty, suddenly felt a tenderness for him and a greater admiration than she had entertained before; and although she harboured no absurd idea of listening to his madness, or of doing anything in the world but laugh at it as it deserved, yet there came on her a strange dislike of the project that she had herself, in sport, suggested: namely, that the smith should be married immediately to the Countess Hilda by the Lord Bishop of Modenstein. The fellow, this smith, had an eye for true beauty, it seemed. It would be hard to tie him down to this dusky, black-maned girl; for so the Princess described the lady whom her brother loved, she herself being, like most of the Elphbergs, rather red than black in color. Accordingly, when the King spoke to her, she said fretfully:

"Am I to be put to refuse the hand of such a fellow as this? Why, to refuse him is a stain on my dignity!" And she looked most haughty.

"Yet you must grant him so much because of his oath," said the King.

"Well, then, I refuse him," said she tartly, and she turned her eyes away from him.

"That is once," said Stephen the smith calmly, and he fixed his eyes on the Princess's face. She felt his gaze, her eyes were drawn back to his, and she exclaimed angrily:

"Yes, I refuse him," and again she looked away. But he looked still more intently at her, waiting for the third refusal.

"It is as easy to say no three times as twice," said the King.

"For a man, sire," murmured Prince Rudolf; for he was very learned in the perilous knowledge of a woman's whims, and, maybe, read something of what was passing in his sister's heart. Certainly he looked at her and laughed, and said to the King:

"Sire, I think this smith is a clever man, for what he really desires is to wed the Countess, and to do it without disobliging my brother. Therefore he professes this ridiculous passion, knowing well that Osra will refuse him, and that he will enjoy the great good fortune of marrying the Countess against his will. Thus he will obey you and be free from my brother's anger. In truth, you're a crafty fellow, Master Stephen!"

"There is no craft, sir," said Stephen. "I have told nothing but the truth."

But the King swore a loud oath, crying:

"Aye, that there is! Rudolf has hit the mark. Yet I do not grudge him his good luck. Refuse him, Osra, and make him happy."

But the dark flush came anew on the Princess's face, for now she did not know whether the smith really loved her or whether he had been making a jest of her in order to save himself in the eyes of her brother Henry, and it became very intolerable to her to suppose that the smith desired the Countess, and had lied in what he said about herself, making a tool of her. Again, it was hardly more tolerable to give him to the Countess, in case he truly loved herself; so that her mind was very greatly disturbed, and she was devoured with eagerness to know the reality of the smith's feelings towards her; for, although he was only a smith yet he was a wonderfully handsome man—in truth, it was curious that she had not paid attention to his looks before. Thus she was reluctant to refuse him a third time, when the Bishop of Modenstein stood there, waiting only for her word to marry him to the Countess; and she rose suddenly from her seat and walked towards the door of the room, and, when she had almost reached the door, she turned her head over her shoulder and cast one smile at Stephen the smith. As she glanced, as the blush again mounted to her face, making her so lovely that her father wondered, and she said in arch softness: "I'll refuse him the third time some other day; two denials are enough for one day," and with that she passed through the door and vanished from their sight.

The King and Rudolf, who had seen the glance that she cast at Stephen, fell to laughing again, swearing to one another that a woman was a woman all the world over, whereat the lips of the Bishop twitched.

"But the marriage can't go on," cried Rudolf at last.

"Let it rest for to-day," said the King, whose anger was past. "Let it rest. The Countess shall be guarded; and, since this young fool" (and he pointed to his son Henry) "will not wander while she is caged, let him go where he will. Then as soon as Osra has refused the smith a third time, we will send for the Bishop."

"And what am I to do, sire?" asked Stephen the smith.

"Why, my son-in-law that would be," chuckled the King, "you may go back to where you came from till I send for you again."

So Stephen, having thanked the King, went back home, and, sitting down to the chasing of a cup, became very thoughtful; for it seemed to him that the Countess had been hardly treated, and that the Prince deserved happiness, and that the Princess was yet more lovely than his eyes had found her before.

Thus, in his work and his meditations, the afternoon wore away fast. So goes time when hand and head are busy.

The Princess Osra walked restlessly up and down the length of her bed-chamber. Dinner was done and it was eight o'clock, and, the season being late October, it had grown dark. She had come thither to be alone; yet, now that she was alone, she could not rest. He was an absurd fellow—that smith! Yes, she thought him fully as handsome as her brother Rudolf. But what did Henry find to love in the black-brown Hilda? She could not understand a man caring for such a colour; a blackamoor would serve as well! Ah, what had that silly smith meant? It must have been a trick, as Rudolf said. Yet when he spoke first of her riding down the street, there was a look in his eyes that a man can hardly put there of his own will. Did the silly fellow then really—? Nay, that was absurd; she prayed that it might not be true, for she would not have the poor fool unhappy. Nay, he was no fool. It was a trick, then! How dared the insolent knave use her for his tricks? Was there no other maiden in Strelsau whose name would have served? Must he lay his tongue to the name of a daughter of the Elphbergs? The fellow deserved flogging, if it were a trick. Ah, was it a trick? Or was it the truth? Oh, in heaven's name, which was it? And the Princess tore the delicate silk of her ivory fan to shreds, and flung the naked sticks with a clatter on the floor.

"I can't rest till I know," she cried, as she came to a stand before a long mirror let into the panel of the wall, and saw herself at full length in it. As she looked a smile came, parting her lips, and she threw her head back as she said: "I will go and ask the smith what he meant." And she smiled again at her own face in triumphant daring; for when she looked, she thought, "I know what he meant! Yet I will hear from himself what he meant."

Stephen the smith sat alone in his house; his apprentices were gone, and he himself neither worked nor supped, but sat still and idle by his hearth. The street was silent also, for it rained and nobody was about. Then suddenly came a light timid rap at the door; so light was it that the smith doubted if he had really heard, but it came again and he rose leisurely and opened the door. Even as he did so a slight tall figure slipped by him, an arm pulled him back, the door was pushed close again, and he was alone inside the house with a lady wrapped in a long riding-cloak, and so veiled that nothing of her face could be seen.

"Welcome, madame," said Stephen the smith; and he drew a chair forward and bowed to his visitor. He was not wearing his apron now, but was dressed in a well-cut suit of brown cloth and had put on a pair of silk stockings. He might have been expecting visitors, so carefully had he arrayed himself.

"Do you know who I am?" asked the veiled lady.

"Since I was a baby, madame," answered the smith, "I have known the sun when I saw it, even though clouds dimmed its face."

A corner of the veil was drawn down, and one eye gleamed in frightened mirth.

"Nobody knows I have come," said Osra. "And you do not know why I have come."

"Is it to answer me for the third time?" asked he, drawing a step nearer, yet observing great deference in his manner.

"It is not to answer at all, but to ask. But I am very silly to have come. What is it to me what you meant?"

"I cannot conceive that it could be anything madame," said Stephen, smiling.

"Yet some think her beautiful—my brother Henry, for example."

"We must respect the opinions of Princes," observed the smith.

"Must we share them?" she asked, drawing the veil yet a little aside.

"We can share nothing—we humble folk—with Princes or Princesses, madame."

"Yet we can make free with their names, though humbler ones would serve as well."

"No other would have served at all, madame."

"Then you meant it?" she cried in sudden half-serious eagerness.

"Nay, but what, madame?"

"I don't care whether you meant it or not."

"Alas! I know it so well, that I marvel you have come to tell me."

The Princess rose and began to walk up and down as she had in her own chamber. Stephen stood regarding her as though God had made his eyes for that one purpose.

"The thing is nothing," she declared petulantly, "but I have a fancy to ask it. Stephen, was it a trick, or—or was it really so? Come, answer me! I can't spend much time on it."

"It is not worth a thought to you. If you say no a third time, all will be well."

"You will marry, the Countess?"

"Can I disobey the King, madame?"

"I am very sorry for her," said the Princess. "A lady of her rank should not be forced to marry a silversmith."

"Indeed I thought so all along. Therefore—"

"You played the trick?" she cried in unmistakable anger.

Stephen made no answer for a time, then he said softly: "If she loves the Prince and he her, why should they not marry?"

"Because his birth is above hers."

"I am glad, then, that I am of no birth, for I can marry whom I will."

"Are you so happy and so free, Stephen?" sighed the Princess; and there was no more of the veil left than served to frame the picture of her face.

"So soon as you have refused me the third time, madame," bowed the smith.

"Will you not answer me?" cried the Princess; and she smiled no more, but was as eager as though she were asking some important question.

"Bring the Countess here to-morrow at this time," said Stephen, "and I will answer."

"You wish, perhaps, to make a comparison between us?" she asked haughtily.

"I cannot be compelled to answer except on my own terms," said the smith. "Yet if you will refuse me once again, the thing will be finished."

"I will refuse you," she cried, "when I please."

"But you will bring the Countess, madame?"

"I am very sorry for her. I have behaved ill to her, Stephen, though I meant only to jest."

"There is room for amends, madame," said he.

The Princess looked long and curiously in his face, but he met her glance with a quiet smile.

"It grows late," said he, "and you should not be here longer, madame. Shall I escort you to the palace?"

"And have every one asking with whom Stephen the smith walks? No, I will go as I came. You have not answered me, Stephen."

"And you have not refused me, madame."

"Will you answer me to-morrow when I come with the Countess?"

"Yes, I will answer then."

The Princess had drawn near to the door; now Stephen opened it for her to pass out; and as she crossed the threshold, she said:

"And I will refuse you then—perhaps;" with which she darted swiftly down the dark, silent, shining street, and was gone; and Stephen, having closed the door, passed his hand twice over his brow, sighed thrice, smiled once, and set about the preparation of his supper.

On the next night, as the Cathedral clock struck nine, there arose a sudden tumult and excitement in the palace. King Henry the Lion was in such a rage as no man had ever seen him in before; even Rudolf, his son, did not dare to laugh at him; courtiers, guards, attendants, lackeys, ran wildly to and fro in immense fear and trepidation. A little later, and a large company of the King's Guard filed out, and, under the command of various officers, scattered themselves through the whole of Strelsau, while five mounted men rode at a gallop to each of the five gates of the city, bearing commands that the gates should be closed, and no man, woman, or child be allowed to pass out without an order under the hand of the King's Marshal. And the King swore by heaven, and by much else, that he would lay them—that is to say, the persons whose disappearance caused all this hubbub—by the heels, and that they should know that there was life in the Lion yet; whereat Prince Rudolf looked as serious as he could contrive to look—for he was wonderfully amused—and called for more wine. And the reason of the whole thing was no other than this, that the room of the Princess Osra was empty, and the room of the Countess Hilda was empty, and nobody had set eyes on Henry, the King's son, for the last two hours or more. Now these facts were, under the circumstances of the case, enough to upset a man of a temper far more equable than was old King Henry the Lion.

Through all the city went the Guards, knocking at every door, disturbing some at their suppers, some from their beds, some in the midst of revelry, some who toiled late for a scanty livelihood. When the doors were not opened briskly, the Guard without ceremony broke them in; they ransacked every crevice and cranny of every house, and displayed the utmost zeal imaginable; nay, one old lady they so terrified that she had a fit there where she lay in bed, and did not recover for the best part of a month. And thus, having traversed all the city and set the whole place in stir and commotion, they came at last to the street where Stephen lived, and to the sign of the "Silver Ship," where he carried on the business bequeathed to him by Aaron Lazarus the Jew.

"Rat, tat, tat!" came thundering on the door from the sword-hilt of the Sergeant in command of the party.

There was no answer; no light shone from the house, for the window was closely shuttered. Again the Sergeant hammered on the door.

"This pestilent smith is gone to bed," he cried in vexation. "But we must leave no house unsearched. Come, we must break in the door!" and he began to examine the door, and found that it was a fine solid door, of good oak and clamped with iron.

"Phew, we shall have a job with this door!" he sighed. "Why, in the devil's name, doesn't the fellow answer? Stephen, Stephen! Ho, there! Stephen!"

Yet no answer came from the inside of the house.

But at this moment another sound struck sharp on the ears of the Sergeant and his men. It was the noise of flames crackling; from the house next to Stephen's (which belonged to him, but was inhabited by a fruit-seller) there welled out smoke in volumes from every window; and the fruit-seller and his family appeared at the windows calling for aid. Seeing this, the Sergeant blew very loudly the whistle that he carried and cried "Fire!" and bade his men run and procure a ladder; for plainly the fruit-seller's house was on fire, and it was a more urgent matter to rescue men and women from burning than to find the Countess and the Prince. Presently the ladder came, and a great crowd of people, roused by the whistle and the cries of fire, came also; and then the door of Stephen's house was opened, and Stephen himself, looking out, asked what was the matter. Being told that the next house was on fire, he turned very grave—for the house was his—and waited for a moment to watch the fruit-seller and his family being brought down the ladder, which task was safely and prosperously accomplished. But the Sergeant said to him: "The fire may well spread, and if there is anyone in your house, it would be prudent to get them out."

"That is well thought of," said Stephen approvingly. "I was working late with three apprentices, and they are still in the house." And he put his head in at his door and called: "You had better come out, lads, the fire may spread." But the Sergeant turned away again and busied himself in putting the fire out.

Then three lads, one being very tall, came out of Stephen's house, clad in their leather breeches, their aprons, and the close-fitting caps that apprentices wore; and for a moment they stood watching the fire at the fruit-seller's. Then, seeing that the fire was burning low—which it did very quickly—they did not stay till the attention of the Sergeant was released from it, but, accompanied by Stephen, turned down the street, and, going along at a brisk rate, rounded the corner and came into the open space in front of the Cathedral.

"The gates will be shut, I fear," said the tallest apprentice. "How came the fire, Stephen?"

"It was three or four trusses of hay, sir, and a few crowns to repair his scorched paint. Shall we go to the gate?"

"Yes, we must try the gate," said Prince Henry, gathering the hand of the Countess into his; and the third apprentice walked silently by Stephen's side. Yet once as she went, she said softly:

"So it was no trick, Stephen?"

"No trick, but the truth, madame," said Stephen.

"I do not know," said Osra, "how I am to return to the palace in these clothes."

"Let us get your brother and the Countess away first," counselled the smith.

Now when they came to the nearest gate it was shut; but at the moment a troop of mounted men rode up, having been sent by the King to scour the country round, in case the fugitives should have escaped already from the city. And the Commandant of the company bore an order from the King's Marshal for the opening of the gate. Seeing this, Stephen the smith went up to him and began to talk to him, the three apprentices standing close by. The Commandant knew Stephen well, and was pleased to talk with him while the gates were opened and the troopers filed through. Stephen kept close by him till the troopers were all through. Then he turned and spoke to the apprentices, and they nodded assent. The Commandant checked his horse for an instant when he was half-way through the gate, and bent down and took Stephen's hand to shake it in farewell. Stephen took his hand with marvellous friendliness, and held it, and would not let him go. But the apprentices edged cautiously nearer and nearer the gate.

"Enough, man, enough!" laughed the Commandant. "We are not parting for ever."

"I trust not, sir, I trust not," said Stephen earnestly, still holding his hand.

"Come, let me go. See, the gate-warden wants to shut the gate!"

"True!" said Stephen. "Good-bye then, sir. Hallo, hallo! stop, stop! Oh, the young rascals!"

For even as Stephen spoke, two of the apprentices had darted through the half-closed gate, and run swiftly forward into the gloom of the night. Stephen swore an oath.

"The rogues!" he cried. "They were to have worked all night to finish an image of Our Lady! And now I shall see no more of them till to-morrow! They shall pay for their prank then, by heaven they shall!" But the Commandant laughed.

"I am sorry I can't catch them for you, friend Stephen," said he, "but I have other fish to fry. Well, boys will be boys. Don't be too hard on them when they return."

"They must answer for what they do," said Stephen; and the Commandant rode on and the gates were shut.

Then the Princess Osra said: "Will they escape, Stephen?"

"They have money in their purses, love in their hearts, and an angry King behind them. I should travel quickly, madame, if I were so placed."

The Princess looked through the grating of the gate.

"Yes," she said, "they have all those. How happy they must be, Stephen! But what am I to do?"

Stephen made no answer and they walked back in silence to his house. It may be that they were wondering whether Prince Henry and the Countess would escape. Yet it may be that they thought of something else. When they reached the house, Stephen bade the Princess go into the inner room and resume her own dress that she might return to the palace, and that it might not be known where she had been nor how she had aided her brother to evade the King's prohibition; and when she, still strangely silent, went in as he bade her, he took his great staff in his hand, and stood on the threshold of the house, his head nearly touching the lintel and his shoulders filling almost all the space between door-post and door-post.

When he had stood there a little while, the same Sergeant of the Guard, recollecting (now that the fire at the fruit-seller's was out) that he had never searched the house of the smith, came again with his four men, and told Stephen to stand aside and allow him to enter the house.

"For I must search it," he said, "or my orders will not be performed."

"Those whom you seek are not here," said Stephen.

"That I must see for myself," answered the Sergeant. "Come, smith, stand aside."

When the Princess heard the voices outside, she put her head round the door of the inner room, and cried in great alarm to Stephen:

"They must not come in, Stephen. At any cost they must not come in!"

"Do not be afraid, madame, they shall not come in," said he.

"I heard a voice in the house," exclaimed the Sergeant.

"It is nothing uncommon to hear in a house," said Stephen, and he grasped more firmly his great staff.

"Will you make way for us?" demanded the Sergeant. "For the last time, will you make way?"

Stephen's eyes kindled; for though he was a man of peace yet his strength was great and he loved sometimes to use it; and above all, he loved to use it now at the bidding and protection of his dear Princess. So he answered the Sergeant from between set teeth:

"Over my dead body you can come in."

Then the Sergeant drew his sword and his men set their halberds in rest, and the Sergeant, crying, "In the King's name!" came at Stephen

STEPHEN STOOD ON THE THRESHOLD
WITH HIS STAFF IN HIS HANDS.

with drawn sword and struck fiercely at him. But Stephen let the great staff drop on the Sergeant's shoulder, and the Sergeant's arm fell powerless by his side. Thereupon the Guards cried aloud, and people began to come out of their houses, seeing that there was a fight at Stephen's door. And Stephen's eyes gleamed, and when the Guards thrust at him, he struck at them, and two of them he stretched senseless on the ground; for his height and reach were such that he struck them before they could come near enough to touch him, and having no fire-arms they could not bring him down.

The Princess, now fully dressed in her own garments, came out into the outer room, and stood there looking at Stephen. Her bosom rose and fell, and her eyes grew dim as she looked; and growing very eager, and being very much moved, she kept murmuring to herself, "I have not said no thrice!" And she spent no thought on the Countess or her brother, nor on how she was to return undetected to the palace, but saw only the figure of Stephen on the threshold, and heard only the cries of the Guards who assaulted him. It seemed to her a brave thing to have such a man to fight for her, and to offer his life to save her shame.

Old King Henry was not a patient man, and when he had waited two hours without news of son, daughter, or Countess, he flew into a mighty passion and sent one for his horse, and another for Rudolf's horse, and a third for Rudolf himself; and he drank a draught of wine, and called to Rudolf to accompany him, that they might see for themselves what the lazy hounds of Guards were doing, that they had not yet come up with the quarry. Prince Rudolf laughed and yawned and wished his brother at the devil, but mounted his horse and rode with the King. Thus they traversed the city, riding swiftly, the old King furiously upbraiding every officer and soldier whom he met; then they rode to the gate; and all the gate-wardens said that nobody had gone out, save that one gate-warden admitted that two apprentices of Stephen the silversmith had contrived to slip out when the gates were open to let the troopers pass. But the King made nothing of it, and, turning with his son, rode up the street where Stephen lived. Here they came suddenly into the midst of a crowd, that filled all the roadway, and would hardly let the horses move even at a foot's pace. The King cried out angrily, "What is this tumult?"

Then the people knew him, and, since common folk are always anxious to serve and commend themselves to the great, a score began all at once to tell him what had happened, some starting with the fire, some going straight to the fight; and the King could not make head or tail of the babel of voices and different stories. And Prince Rudolf dropped his reins and sat on his horse laughing. But the King, his patience being clean gone, drew his sword and cried fiercely, "Make way!" and set his spurs to his horse, not recking whether he hurt any man in life or limb. Thus he gained a passage through the crowd, and came near to Stephen's house, Prince Rudolf following in his wake, still greatly amused at all that was happening.

But the sight they saw there arrested even Prince Rudolf's smiles, and he raised himself in his stirrups with a sudden cry of wonder. For four more of the Guard had come, and there were now six standing round the doorway, and three lay stretched on the ground; but Stephen the smith still stood on the threshold, with his staff in his hand. Blood flowed from a wound in his head, but he twirled the staff to and fro, and was not weary, and none of the Guard dared to rush in and close with him. Thus he had held the threshold for an hour; yet the Princess Osra could not escape unless he could drive off the Guard for a few moments, and this he hoped to do, thinking that they might draw off and wait for reinforcements; but in any case he had sworn that they should not pass. And Osra did not pray him to let them pass, but stood motionless in the middle of the room behind him, her hands clasped, her face rigid, and her eyes all aflame with admiration of his strength and his courage.

Thus matters were when the old King and Prince Rudolf broke through the crowd that ringed the house round, and the King cried out, asking what was the meaning of all that he saw.

But when the King heard that Stephen the smith resisted the officers, would not suffer his house to be searched, had stretched three of the Guards senseless on the ground, and still more than held his own, he fell into a great rage; he roared out on them all, calling them cowards, and, before his son or any one else could stop him, he drew his sword, and dug his spurs into his horse; the horse bounded forward and knocked down one of the Guards who stood round Stephen. Then the King, neither challenging Stephen to yield, nor giving him time to stand aside, being carried away by passion, raised his sword and rode full at him. And the Princess from within caught sight of his face, and she fell on her knees with a moan and hid her face. Then Stephen saw that it was the King and none other who rode against him; and even had the King given him time, it may be that he would not have yielded, for he was a very resolute man, and he had pledged his promise to Osra the Princess. But he had no time for thought, for the King was on him in the space of a second, and he could do nothing but drop the staff that he held, and stand defenceless in the doorway; for he would neither strike the King nor yield the passage. But the King, in his fury not heeding that Stephen had dropped his staff, drew back his arm and lunged with his sword, and thrust the smith through the chest; and Stephen reeled and fell on one knee, and his blood flowed out on the stone of the doorstep. Then the King reined in his horse, and sat looking down on Stephen; but Rudolf leapt to the ground, and came and caught hold of Stephen, supporting him, and asking, "What does it mean, man, what does it mean?"

Then Stephen, being very faint with his wound, said with difficulty: "Come in alone—you and the King alone."

Prince Rudolf looked at the King, who sheathed his sword and dismounted from his horse; the Prince supported Stephen inside the house, and the King followed them, shutting the door on all the people outside.

Then King Henry saw his daughter, crouching now in the middle of the room, her face hidden in her hands. Surprise and wonder banished his rage and he could not do more than gasp her name, while the Prince, who knelt supporting Stephen, cried to her, asking how she came there; but she answered nothing. She took her hands from her face and looked at Stephen; and when she saw that he was hurt and bleeding, she fell to sobbing and hid her face again. And she did not know whether she would have him live or die; for if he lived he could not be hers, and if he died her heart would ache sorely for him. Then Stephen, being supported by the arms of Prince Rudolf, made shift to speak, and he told the King how, at his persuasion, the Princess had brought the Countess thither; how he himself had contrived the presence of the Prince at the same time, how again the Princess had been prevailed upon to aid the lovers; how they assumed the disguise of apprentices; and how, hearing the arrival of the Guard, they had escaped out into the street; and lastly, how that the Prince and the Countess had got out of the city. But he said nothing of the fire at the fruit-sellers's, nor of how he himself had bribed the fruit-seller to set the hay on fire, speaking to him from the back windows of the house, and flinging a purse of gold pieces across to him; nor did this ever become known to the King. And when Stephen had said his say, he fell back very faint in the arms of the Prince; and the Prince tore a scarf from his waist, and tried to staunch the blood from Stephen's wound. But the old King, who was a hard man, smiled grimly.

"Indeed he has tricked us finely, this smith, and he is a clever fellow," said he; "but unless he would rather hang than bleed to death, let his wound be, Rudolf. For by heaven, if you cure him, I will hang him."

"Do not be afraid, sire," said Stephen; "the Prince cannot cure me. You strike straight, though you are hard on seventy."

"Straight enough for a rascal like you," said the King well pleased; and he added, "Hold the fellow easily, Rudolf, I would not have him suffer." And this was, they say, the only time in all his life that Henry the Lion shewed a sign of pity to any man.

But Stephen was now very faint, and he cast his eyes towards the Princess; and Rudolf followed his eyes. Now Rudolf had an affection for Stephen, and he loved his sister, and was a man of soft heart; so he cried gently to Osra, "Come, sister, and help me with him." And she rose, and came and sat down by the wall, and gathered Stephen's head into her lap; and there he lay, looking up at her, with a smile on his lips. But still he bled, and his blood stained the white cloak that she wore over her robe; and her tears dropped on his face. But Rudolf took his father by the arm, and led him a little way off, saying:

"What matter, sire? The girl is young, and the man is dying. Let them be."

The old King, grumbling, let himself be led away; and perhaps even he was moved, for he forgot Prince Henry and the Countess, and did not think of sending men in pursuit of them, for which reason they obtained a fair and long start in their flight.

Then Stephen, looking up at Osra said:

"Do not weep, madame. They will escape now, and they will be happy."

"I was not weeping for them," said the Princess.

Stephen was silent for a little, and then he said:

"In very truth it was no trick, madame; it was even as I said, from the first day that you rode along the street here; it was always the same in my heart, and would always have been, however long I had lived."

"I do not doubt it, Stephen; and it is not for doubt of it that I weep," said she.

Then, after a little while, he said:

"Do you weep, madame, because I am dying?"

"Yes, I weep for that."

"Would you have me live, madame?" he asked.

"No, I would not—no—but I do not know," she said.

Then Stephen the smith smiled, and his smile was happy.

"Yet," said he, "it would make small difference to the Princess Osra whether Stephen the smith lived or died."

At this, although he lay there a dying man, a sudden flush of red spread all over her cheeks, and she turned her eyes away from his, and would not meet his glance; she made him no answer, and he said again:

"What can it concern the Princess whether I live or die?"

Still the blush burnt on her check, and still she had no answer to give to Stephen as he lay dying with his head on her lap. And a bright gleam came into his eyes, and he tried to move a hand towards her hand; and she, seeing the effort, put out her hand and held his; and he whispered very low, for he could hardly, speak:

"You have not yet refused me three times, madame."

At that her eyes came back to his, and their eyes dwelt long on one another. And for a moment it seemed to them that all things became possible, life and joy and love. Yet since all could not be, they were content that none should be.

Then the Princess bent low over his head, and she whispered to him:

"No, I have not refused you thrice, Stephen."

His lips just moved once again, and, being very near him, she heard:

"And you will not?" he said.

"No," said she, and she kissed his lips, and he smiled and turned on his side; and he nestled his head, as it were cosily, on her lap, and he said no more.

Thus died Stephen the silversmith of Strelsau, happy in his death because Osra the Princess had not refused him thrice. And she laid him gently on the ground, and rose, and went across to where the King sat with Rudolf.

"Sire, he is dead," said she.

"It is well," said the King. And he bade Rudolf go and cause all the people to leave the streets, and return to their houses; and when all the streets were cleared, the Princess veiled herself, and her brother mounted her on his horse, and thus she rode back to the palace; and none knew that she had been in the house of Stephen the silversmith.

And after many months Prince Henry, who had made good his escape and married the lady whom he loved, was reconciled to his father and returned to the city of Strelsau. And when he heard how Stephen had died, he raised a stately monument over him, and had carved on it his name, and the day and year in which he had died; and underneath he caused to be engraved the words, "From a Friend to a Friend." But when this monument had stood three days in its place, there came thither a lady closely veiled; she prayed on her knees by the monument for a long while, and then rose and stood regarding it; and her eyes rested on the last words that Prince Henry had written on the stone. Then she came nearer, and kissed the words, and. when she had kissed them, she whispered softly, "From a Lover to a Lover"; and, having whispered this, she turned away and went back to the palace, and came no more to the tomb, for fear that the people should remark her coming. Yet often in the days that followed she would open the window of her bed-chamber by night, and she would whisper to the silent trusty darkness, that holds secrets and comforts sore hearts:

"Not thrice, Stephen, not thrice!"

Therefore it may be that there had been a sweet madness in her heart, and that Stephen the silversmith had done a great thing, a thing that would appear impossible, before he died. And, as Prince Rudolf said, what matter? For the girl was young, and the dream was sweet, and the man was dead, and in death at last are all men equal.

Chapter II

The Wager of the Marquis de Mérosailles

In the year 1734, as spring began, there arrived at Strelsau a French nobleman of high rank and great possessions, endowed also with many accomplishments. He came to visit Prince Rudolf, whose acquaintance he had made while the Prince was at Paris in the course of his travels. King Henry received M. de Mérosailles—for such was his name— most graciously, and sent a guard of honour to conduct him to the Castle of Zenda, where the Prince was then staying in company with his sister Osra. There the Marquis, on his arrival, was greeted with much joy by Prince Rudolf, who found his sojourn in the country somewhat irksome and was glad of the society of a friend with whom he could talk, and sport, and play at cards. All these things he did with M. de Mérosailles, and a great friendship arose between the young men, so that they spoke very freely to one another at all times, and most of all when they had drunk their wine and sat together in the evening in Prince Rudolf's chamber that looked across the moat towards the gardens; for the new *château* that now stands on the site of these gardens was not then built. And one night M. de Mérosailles made bold to ask the Prince how it fell out that his sister the Princess, a lady of such great beauty, seemed sad, and shewed no pleasure in the society of any gentleman, but treated all alike with coldness and disdain. Prince Rudolf, laughing, answered that girls were strange creatures, and that he had ceased to trouble his head about them (of his heart he said nothing) and he finished by exclaiming: "On my honour, I doubt if she so much as knows you are here, for she has not looked at you once since your arrival!" And he smiled maliciously, for he knew that the Marquis was not accustomed to be neglected by ladies, and would take it ill that even a Princess should be unconscious of his presence. In this he calculated rightly, for M. de Mérosailles was greatly vexed, and, twisting his glass in his fingers, he said:

"If she were not a Princess, and your sister, sir, I would engage to make her look at me."

"I am not hurt by her looking at you," rejoined the Prince: for that evening he was very merry. "A look is no great thing."

The Marquis, being no less merry, and knowing that Rudolf had not the regard for his dignity that a Prince should have, threw out carelessly:

"A kiss is more, Sir."

"It is a great deal more," laughed the Prince, tugging his moustache.

"Are you ready for a wager, Sir?" asked M. de Mérosailles, leaning across the table towards him.

"I'll lay you a thousand crowns to a hundred that you do not gain a kiss, using what means you will, save force."

"I'll take that wager, sir," cried the Marquis. "But it shall be three, not one."

"Have a care," said the Prince. "Don't go too near the flame, my lord! There are some wings in Strelsau singed at that candle."

"Indeed the light is very bright," assented the Marquis courteously. "That risk I must run, though, if I am to win my wager. It is to be three then, and by what means I will, save force?"

"Even so," said Rudolf, and he laughed again. For he thought the wager harmless, since by no device could M. de Mérosailles win so much as one kiss from the Princess Osra, and the wager stood at three. But he did not think how he wronged his sister by using her name lightly, being in all such matters a man of careless mind.

But the Marquis, having made his wager, set himself steadily to win it. Therefore he brought forth the choicest clothes from his wardrobe, and ornaments, and perfumes; and he laid fine presents at the Princess's feet; and he waylaid her wherever she went, and was profuse of glances, sighs, and hints; and he wrote sonnets, as fine gentlemen used in those days, and lyrics and pastorals, wherein she figured under charming names. These he bribed the Princess's waiting-women to leave in their mistress's chamber. Moreover he looked now sorrowful, now passionate, and he ate nothing at dinner, but drank his wine in wild gulps, as though he sought to banish sadness. So that, in a word, there was no device in Cupid's armoury that the Marquis de Mérosailles did not practise in the endeavour to win a look from the Princess Osra. But no look came, and he got nothing from her but cold civility. Yet she had looked at him when he looked not—for Princesses are much like other maidens—and thought him a very pretty gentleman, and was highly amused by his extravagance. Yet she did not believe it to witness any true devotion to her, but thought it mere gallantry.

Then, one day M. de Mérosailles, having tried all else that he could think of, took to his bed. He sent for a physician, and paid him a high fee to find the seeds of a rapid and fatal disease in him: and he made his body-servant whiten his face and darken his room; and he groaned very pitifully, saying that he was sick, and that he was glad of it; for death would be better far than the continued disdain of the Princess Osra. And all this, being told by the Marquis's servants to the Princess's waiting-women, reached Osra's ears, and caused her much perturbation. For she now perceived that the passion of the Marquis was real and deep, and she became very sorry for him: the longer the face of the rascally physician grew, the more sad the Princess became: she walked up and down, bewailing the terrible effects of her beauty, wishing that she were not so fair, and mourning very tenderly for the sad plight of the unhappy Marquis.

Through all Prince Rudolf looked on, but was bound by his wager not to undeceive her; moreover he found much entertainment in the matter, and swore that it was worth three times a thousand crowns.

At last the Marquis sent by the mouth of his physician a very humble and pitiful message to the Princess, in which he spoke of himself as near to death, hinted at the cruel cause of his condition, and prayed her of compassion to visit him in his chamber, and speak a word of comfort, or at least let him look on her face: for the brightness of her eyes, he said, might cure even what it had caused.

Deceived by this appeal, Princess Osra agreed to go; moved by some strange impulse, she put on her choicest array, dressed her hair most splendidly, and came into the chamber looking like a goddess. There lay the Marquis, white as a ghost and languid on his pillows; and they were left, as they thought, alone. Then Osra sat down and began to talk very gently and kindly to him, glancing only at the madness which brought him to his sad state, and imploring him to summon his resolution, and conquer his sickness for his friends' sake at home in France, and for the sake of her brother, who loved him.

THE PHYSICIAN RECEIVES PRINCESS OSRA.

"There is nobody who loves me," said the Marquis petulantly; and when Osra cried out at this, he went on, "For the love of those whom I do not love is nothing to me, and the only soul alive I love—" There he stopped, but his eyes, fixed on Osra's face, ended the sentence for him. And she blushed, and looked away. Then thinking the moment was come, he burst suddenly into a flood of protestations and self-reproach, cursing himself for a fool and a presumptuous madman, pitifully craving her pardon, and declaring that he did not deserve her kindness, and yet that he could not live without it, and that anyhow he would be dead soon, and thus cease to trouble her. But she, being thus passionately assailed, showed such sweet tenderness and compunction and pity, that M. de Mérosailles came very near to forgetting that he was playing a comedy, and threw himself into his part with eagerness, redoubling his vehemence, and feeling now full half of what he said. For the Princess was to his eyes far more beautiful in her softer mood. Yet he remembered his wager, and, at last, when she was nearly in tears and ready, as it seemed, to do anything to give him comfort, he cried desperately:

"Ah, leave, leave me! Leave me to die alone! Yet, for pity's sake, before you go, and before I die, give me your forgiveness, and let your lips touch my forehead in token of it. Then I shall die in peace."

At that the Princess blushed still more, and her eyes were wet, and shone, for she was deeply touched at his misery and at the sad prospect of the death for love of so gallant a gentleman. Thus she could scarcely speak for emotion; and the Marquis seeing her emotion was himself deeply affected; and she rose from her chair, and bent over him, and whispered comfort to him. Then she leant down, and very lightly touched his forehead with her lips; he felt her eyelashes, which were wet with tears, brush the skin of his forehead; and then she sobbed and covered her face with her hands. Indeed his state seemed to her most pitiful.

Thus M. de Mérosailles had won one of his three kisses; yet, strange to tell, there was no triumph in him, but now he perceived the baseness of his device; and the sweet kindness of the Princess, working together with the great beauty of her softened manner, so affected him that he thought no more of his wager and could not endure to carry on his deception; nothing would serve his turn but to confess to the Princess what he had done, humbling himself in the dust before her, and entreating her to pardon him and let him find forgiveness.

Impelled by these feelings, after he had lain still a few moments listening to the Princess weeping, he leapt suddenly out of bed, showing himself fully dressed under the bed-gown which he now eagerly tore off; and he rubbed all the white he could from his checks, and then he fell on his knees before the Princess, crying to her that he had played the meanest trick on her, and that he was a scoundrel, and no gentleman, and that unless she forgave him he should in very truth die; nay, that he would not consent to live unless he could win from her pardon for his deceit. And in all this he was now absolutely in earnest, wondering only how he had not been as passionately enamoured of her from the first as he had feigned himself to be. For a man in love can never conceive himself out of it, nor he that is out of it in it; for if he can, he is halfway to the one or the other, however little he may know it.

At first the Princess sat as though she were turned to stone: but when he finished his confession, and she understood the trick that had been played on her, and how not only her kiss, but also her tears, had been won from her by fraud, and when she thought, as she did, that the Marquis was playing another trick on her, and that there was no more truth or honesty in his present protestations than in those which went before, she fell into great shame and into a great rage; her eyes flashed like the eyes of her father himself, as she rose to her feet and looked down on M. de Mérosailles as he knelt imploring her. Now her face turned pale from red, and she set her lips, and she drew her gown close round her, lest his touch should defile it (so the unhappy gentleman understood her gesture) and she picked her steps daintily round him, for fear she should happen to come in contact with so foul a thing. Thus she walked to the door, and, having reached it, she turned and said to him:

"Your death may blot out the insult—nothing less." And with her head held high, and her whole air full of scorn, she swept out of the room, leaving the Marquis on his knees. He started up to follow her, but dared not; he flung himself on the bed in a paroxysm of shame and vexation, and now of love also, and he cried out loud:

"Then my death shall blot it out, since nothing else will serve!"

He was in a desperate mood. For a long time he lay there, and then, having risen, dressed himself in a sombre suit of black, and buckled his sword by his side, and, having put on his riding boots and summoned his servant, bade him saddle his horse. "For," said he to himself, "I will ride into the forest, and there kill myself; and perhaps when I am dead the Princess will forgive, and will believe in my love, and grieve a little for me."

Now as he went from his chamber to cross the moat by the drawbridge, he encountered Prince Rudolf returning from hawking. They met full in the centre of the bridge, and the Prince, seeing M. de Mérosailles dressed all in black from the feather in his hat to his boots, called out mockingly:

"Who is to be buried to-day, my lord, and whither do you ride to the funeral? It cannot be yourself, for I see that you are marvellously recovered of your sickness."

"But it is myself," answered the Marquis, coming near, and speaking low that the servants and the falconers might not overhear. "I ride, sir, to my own funeral."

"The jest is still afoot, then?" asked the Prince. "Yet I do not see my sister at the window to watch you go, and I warrant you have made no way with your wager yet."

"A thousand curses on my wager!" cried the Marquis. "Yes, I have made way with the accursed thing, and that is why I now go to my death."

"What, has she kissed you?" cried the Prince, with a merry astonished laugh.

"Yes, sir, she has kissed me once, and therefore I go to die."

"I have heard of many a better reason, then," answered the Prince.

By now the Prince had dismounted, and he stood by M. de Mérosailles in the middle of the bridge, and heard from him how the trick had prospered. At this he was much tickled, and, alas, he was even more diverted when the penitence of the Marquis was revealed to him, and was most of all moved to merriment when it appeared that the Marquis, having gone too near the candle, had been caught by its flame, and was so terribly singed and scorched that he could not bear to live. And while they talked on the bridge the Princess looked out on them from a lofty narrow window, but neither of them saw her. But when the Prince had done laughing, he put his arm through his friend's and bade him not be a fool, but come in and toast the Princess's kiss in a draught of wine. "For," he said, "though you will never get the other two, yet it is a brave exploit to have got one."

But the Marquis shook his head, and his air was so resolute, and so full of sorrow, that not only was Rudolf alarmed for his reason, but Princess Osra also, at the window, wondered what ailed him and why he wore such a long face; and now she noticed that he was dressed all in black, and that his horse waited for him across the bridge.

"Not," said she, "that I care what becomes of the impudent rogue!" Yet she did not leave the window, but watched very intently to see what M. de Mérosailles would do.

For a long while he talked with Rudolf on the bridge, Rudolf seeming more serious than he was wont to be; and at last the Marquis bent to kiss the Prince's hand, and the Prince raised him and kissed him on either cheek; then the Marquis went and mounted his horse, and rode off, slowly and unattended, into the glades of the forest of Zenda; but the Prince, with a shrug of the shoulders and a frown on his brow, entered under the portcullis, and disappeared from his sister's view.

Upon this the Princess, assuming an air of great carelessness, walked down from the room where she was, and found her brother, sitting still in his boots and drinking wine; and she said:

"M. de Mérosailles has taken his leave then?"

"Even so, madame," rejoined Rudolf.

Then she broke into a fierce attack on the Marquis, and on her brother also; for a man, said she, is known by his friends, and what a man Rudolf must be to have a friend like the Marquis de Mérosailles!

"Most brothers," she said in fiery temper, "would make him answer for what he has done with his life. But you laugh, nay, I daresay you had a hand in it."

As to this last charge the Prince had the discretion to say nothing; he chose rather to answer the first part of what she said, and shrugging his shoulders again rejoined:

"The fool saves me the trouble, for he has gone off to kill himself."

"To kill himself?" she said, half incredulous, but also half believing, because of the Marquis's gloomy looks and black clothes.

"To kill himself," repeated Rudolf. "For in the first place you are angry, so he cannot live; in the second he has behaved like a rogue, so he cannot live; and in the third place you are so lovely, sister, that he cannot live; and in the first, second, and third places he is a fool, so he cannot live." And the Prince finished his flagon of wine with every sign of ill-humour in his manner.

"He is well dead," she cried.

"Oh, as you please," said he. "He is not the first brave man who has died on your account." And he rose and strode out of the room very surlily; for he had a great friendship for M. de Mérosailles, and had no patience with men who let love make dead bones of them.

The Princess Osra, being left alone, sat for a little time in deep thought. There rose before her mind the picture of M. de Mérosailles riding mournfully through the gloom of the forest to his death. And although his conduct had been all and more than all that she had called it, yet it seemed hard that he should die for it. Moreover, if he now in truth felt what he had before feigned, the present truth was an atonement for the past treachery; and she said to herself that she could not sleep quietly that night if the Marquis killed himself in the forest. Presently she wandered slowly up to her chamber, and looked in the mirror, and murmured low, "Poor fellow!" and then with sudden speed she attired herself for riding, and commanded her horse to be saddled, and darted down the stairs and across the bridge, and mounted, and, forbidding any one to accompany her, rode away into the forest, following the marks of the hoofs of M. de Mérosailles's horse. It was then late afternoon, and the slanting rays of the sun, striking through the tree-trunks, reddened her face as she rode along, spurring her horse, and following hard on the track of the forlorn gentleman. But what she intended to do if she came up with him she did not think.

When she had ridden an hour or more, she saw his horse tethered to a trunk; and there was a ring of trees and bushes near, encircling an open grassy spot. Herself dismounting, and fastening her horse by the Marquis's horse, she stole up, and saw M. de Mérosailles sitting on the ground, his drawn sword lying beside him; and his back was towards her. She held her breath and waited a few moments. Then he took up the sword and felt the point and also the edge of it, and sighed deeply; and the Princess thought that this sorrowful mood became him better than any she had seen him in before. Then he rose to his feet, and took his sword by the blade beneath the hilt, and turned the point of it towards his heart. But Osra, fearing that the deed would be done immediately, called out eagerly, "My lord, my lord!" and M. de Mérosailles turned round with a great start. When he saw her, he stood in astonishment, his hand still holding the blade of the sword. And, standing just on the other side of the trees, she said:

"Is your offence against me to be cured by adding an offence against Heaven and the Church?"

And she looked on him with great severity, yet her cheek was flushed, and after a while she did not meet his glance.

"How came you here, madame?" he asked in wonder.

She saw M. de Mérosailles sitting on the ground.

"I heard," she said, "that you meditated this great sin, and I rode after you to forbid it."

"Can you forbid what you cause?" he asked.

"I am not the cause of it," she said, "but your own trickery."

"It is true. I am not worthy to live," cried the Marquis, smiting the hilt of his sword on the ground. "I pray you, madame, leave me alone to die. For I cannot tear myself from the world so long as I see your face." And as he spoke he knelt on one knee, as though he were doing homage to her.

The Princess caught at the bough of the tree under which she stood, and pulled the bough down, so that its leaves half hid her face, and the Marquis saw little more than her eyes from among the foliage. Thus being better able to speak to him, she said softly:

"And dare you die, unforgiven?"

"I had prayed for forgiveness before you found me, madame," said he.

"Of heaven, my lord?"

"Of heaven, madame. For of heaven I dare to ask it."

The bough swayed up and down; now Osra's gleaming hair, and now her cheek, and always her eyes were seen through the leaves. And presently the Marquis heard a voice asking:

"Does heaven forgive unasked?"

"Indeed, no," he said, wondering.

"And," she said, "are we poor mortals kinder than heaven?"

The Marquis rose, and took a step or two towards where the bough swayed up and down, and then knelt again.

"A great sinner," said he, "cannot believe himself forgiven."

"Then he wrongs the power of which he seeks forgiveness; for forgiveness is divine."

"Then I will ask it, and, if I obtain it, I shall die happy."

Again the bough swayed; and Osra said:

"Nay, if you will die, you may die unforgiven."

M. de Mérosailles hearing these words sprang to his feet, and came towards the bough, until he was so close that he touched the green leaves; through them the eyes of Osra gleamed: the sun's rays struck on her eyes, and they danced in the sun; and her cheeks were reddened by the same or some other cause. And the evening was very still, and there were no sounds in the forest.

"I cannot believe that you forgive. The crime is so great," said he.

"It was great; yet I forgive."

"I cannot believe it," said he again, and he looked at the point of his sword, and then he looked through the leaves at the Princess.

"I cannot do more than say that if you will live, I will forgive. And we will forget."

"By heaven, no," he whispered. "If I must forget to be forgiven, then I will remember and be unforgiven."

The faintest laugh reached him from among the foliage.

"Then I will forget, and you shall be forgiven," said she.

The Marquis put up his hand, and held a leaf aside, and he said again:

"I cannot believe myself forgiven. Is there no token of forgiveness?"

"Pray, my lord, do not put the leaves aside."

"I still must die, unless I have sure warrant of forgiveness."

"Ah, you try to make me think that!"

"By heaven, it is true!" And again he pointed his sword at his heart, and he swore on his honour that unless she gave him a token he would still kill himself.

"Oh," said the Princess with great petulance, "I wish I had not come!"

"Then I should have been dead by now—dead, unforgiven."

"But you will still die!"

Yes, I must still die, unless—"

"Sheathe your sword, my lord. The sun strikes it, and it dazzles my eyes."

"That cannot be: for your eyes are brighter than sun and sword together."

"Then I must shade them with the leaves."

"Yes, shade them with the leaves," he whispered. "Madame, is there no token of forgiveness?"

In the silence that followed his eyes spoke, at last she said:

"Why did you swear on your honour?"

"Because it is an oath that I cannot break."

"Indeed I wish that I had not come," sighed Princess Osra.

Again came silence. The bough was pressed down for an instant; then it swayed swiftly up again; and its leaves brushed the cheek of M. de Mérosailles. And he laughed loudly and joyfully.

"Something touched my cheek," said he.

"It must have been a leaf," said Princess Osra.

"Ah, a leaf!"

"I think so," said Princess Osra.

"Then it was a leaf of the Tree of Life," said M. de Mérosailles.

"I wish some one would set me on my horse," said Osra.

"That you may ride back to the castle alone?"

"Yes, unless you would relieve my brother's anxiety."

"It would be courteous to do that much," said the Marquis.

So they mounted, and rode back through the forest.

In an hour the Princess had come, and in the space of something over two hours they returned; yet during all this time they spoke hardly a word; and although the sun was now set, yet the glow remained on the face and in the eyes of Princess Osra; while M. de Mérosailles, being forgiven, rode with a smile on his lips.

But when they came to the castle, Prince Rudolf ran out to meet them, and he cried almost before he reached them:

"Hasten, hasten! There is not a moment to lose, if the Marquis values life or liberty!" And when he came to them he told them that a waiting-woman had been false to M. de Mérosailles and, after taking his money, had hid herself in his chamber, and seen the first kiss that the Princess gave him, and, having made some pretext to gain a holiday, had gone to the King, who was hunting near, and betrayed the whole matter to him.

"And one of my gentlemen," he continued, "has ridden here to tell me. In an hour the Guards will be here, and if the King catches you, my lord, you will hang as sure as I live."

The Princess turned very pale, but M. de Mérosailles said haughtily, "I ask your pardon, sir, but the King dares not hang me. For I am a gentleman and a subject of the King of France."

"Man, man!" cried Rudolf. "The Lion will hang you first, and think of all that afterwards! Come now, it is dusk. You shall dress yourself as my groom, and I will ride to the frontier, and you shall ride behind me, and thus you may get safe away. I cannot have you hanged over such a trifle."

"I would have given my life willingly for what you call a trifle, sir," said the Marquis with a bow to Osra.

"Then have the trifle and life too," said Rudolf derisively. "Come in with me, and I will give you your livery!"

When the Prince and M. de Mérosailles came out again on the drawbridge the evening had fallen, and it was dark; their horses stood at the end of the bridge, and by the horses stood the Princess.

"Quick!" said she. "For a peasant who came in, bringing a load of wood, saw a troop of men coming over the crown of the hill, and he says they are the King's Guard."

"Mount, man!" cried the Prince to M. de Mérosailles, who was now dressed as a groom. "Perhaps we can get clear, or perhaps they will not dare to stop me."

But the Marquis hesitated a little, for he did not like to run away; but the Princess ran a little forward and, shading her eyes with her hand, cried, "See there! I see the gleam of steel in the dark. They have reached the top of the hill, and are riding down."

Then Prince Rudolf sprang on his horse, calling again to M. de Mérosailles, "Quick, quick! Your life hangs on it!"

Then at last the Marquis, though he was most reluctant to depart, was about to spring on his horse, when the Princess turned and glided back swiftly to them. And—let it be remembered that evening had fallen thick and black—she came to her brother and put out her hand, and grasped his hand, and said:

"My lord, I forgive your wrong, and I thank you for your courtesy, and I wish you farewell."

Prince Rudolf, astonished, gazed at her without speaking. But she, moving very quickly in spite of the darkness, ran to where M. de Mérosailles was about to spring on his horse, and she flung one arm lightly about his neck, and she said:

"Farewell, dear brother, God preserve you. See that no harm comes to my good friend, M. de Mérosailles." And she kissed him lightly on the cheek. Then she suddenly gave a loud cry of dismay, exclaiming "Alas, what have I done? Ah, what have I done?" and she hid her face in her two hands.

Prince Rudolf burst into a loud short laugh, yet he said nothing to his sister, but again urged the Marquis to mount his horse. And the Marquis, who was in a sad tumult of triumph and of woe, leapt up; and they rode out, and turning their faces towards the forest, set spurs to their horses and vanished at a breakneck speed into the glades. And no sooner were they gone than the troopers of the King's Guard clattered at a canter up to the end of the bridge, where the Princess Osra stood. But when their captain saw the Princess, he drew rein.

"What is your errand, sir?" she asked most coldly and haughtily.

"Madame, we are ordered to bring the Marquis de Mérosailles alive or dead into the King's presence, and we have information that he is in the castle, unless, indeed, he were one of the horsemen who rode away just now."

"The horsemen you saw were my brother the Prince and his groom," said Osra. "But if you think that M. de Mérosailles is in the castle, pray search the castle from keep to cellar; and if you find him, carry him to my father, according to your orders."

Then the troopers dismounted in great haste, and ransacked the castle from keep to cellar; and they found the clothes of the Marquis, and the white powder with which he had whitened his face, but the Marquis they did not find. So the captain came again to the Princess, who still stood at the end of the bridge, and said:

"Madame, he is not in the castle."

"Is he not?" said she and turned away, and, walking to the middle of the bridge, looked down into the water of the moat.

"Was it in truth the Prince's groom who rode with him, madame?" asked the captain, following her.

"In truth, sir, it was so dark," answered the Princess, "that I could not myself clearly distinguish the man's face."

"One was the Prince, for I saw you embrace him, madame."

"You do well to conclude that that was my brother," said Osra, smiling a little.

"And to the other, madame, you gave your hand."

"And now I give it to you," said she with haughty insolence. "And if to my father's servant, why not to my brother's?" And she held out her hand that he might kiss it, and turned away from him, and looked down into the water again.

"But we found M.. de Mérosailles's clothes in the castle!" persisted the captain.

"He may well have left something of his in the castle," said the Princess.

"I will ride after them!" cried the captain.

"I doubt if you will catch them," smiled the Princess; for by now the pair had been gone half an hour, and the frontier was but ten miles from the castle, and they could not be overtaken. Yet the captain rode off with his men, and pursued till he met Prince Rudolf returning alone, having seen de Mérosailles safe on his way. And Rudolf had paid the sum of a thousand crowns to the Marquis, so that the fugitive was well provided for his journey and travelling with many relays of horses, made good his escape from the clutches of King Henry.

But the Princess Osra stayed a long time looking down at the water in the moat. Sometimes she sighed, and then, again she frowned, and, although nobody was there, and it was very dark into the bargain, more than once she blushed. And at last she turned to go into the castle. But as she went, she murmured softly to herself:

"Why I kissed him the first time I know; it was in pity. And why I kissed him the second time I know; it was in forgiveness. But why I kissed him the third time, or what that kiss meant," said Osra, "heaven knows."

And she went in with a smile on her lips.

Chapter III

The Madness of Lord Harry Culverhouse

"Seeing that my father Henry is dead, and that I am King; seeing also that I am no longer a bachelor, but a married man"—and here he bowed to Margaret of Tuscany, his newly wedded wife; "and seeing that Osra's turned twenty years of age—why, we are all to be sober folk at Strelsau from this day forward, and we are to play no more pranks. Here's a pledge to it!"

And having said this, King Rudolf III took a deep draught of wine.

At this moment the ushers announced that the Lord Harry Culverhouse had come to take his leave of their Majesties and of the Princess. This gentleman had accompanied the Embassy that came from England to congratulate the King on his marriage, and he had stayed some months in Strelsau, very eagerly acceding to the King's invitation to prolong his visit. For such were his folly and headstrong passion, that he had fallen most desperately in love with the fair face of Princess Osra, and could not endure to live out of her presence. Yet now he came to bid farewell, and when he was ushered in, Rudolf received him with much graciousness, and made him a present of his own miniature set in diamonds, while the Queen gave him her miniature set in the lid of a golden casket. In return, Lord Harry prayed the King to accept a richly mounted sword, and the Queen an ivory fan, painted by the greatest artist of France and bearing her cipher in jewels. Then he came to Princess Osra, and she, having bidden him farewell, said:

"I am a poor maid, my lord, and I can give no great gift, but take this pin from my hair and keep it for my sake."

And she drew out a golden pin from her hair, a long and sharp pin, bearing for its head her cipher in brilliants, and she gave it to him, smiling.

But he, bowing low and then falling on his knee, offered her a box of red morocco leather, and when she opened it she saw a necklace of rubies of great splendour. The Princess flushed red, seeing that the gift was most costly. And she would fain have refused it, and held it out again to Lord Harry. But he turned swiftly away, and, bowing once more, withdrew. Then the Princess said to her brother, "It is too costly."

The King, seeing how splendid the gift was, frowned a little, and then said:

"He must be a man of very great wealth. They are rich in England. I am sorry the gift is so great, but we cannot refuse it without wounding his honour."

So the Princess set the ruby necklace with her other jewels, and thought for a day or two that Lord Harry was no wiser than other men, and then forgot him.

Now Lord Harry Culverhouse, on leaving the King's presence, had mounted his horse, which was a fine charger and splendidly equipped, and ridden alone out of Strelsau; for he had dismissed all his servants and despatched them with suitable gratuities to their own country. He rode through the afternoon, and in the evening he reached a village fifteen miles away; here he stopped at a cottage, and an old man came out and escorted him in. A bundle lay on the table in the little parlour of the cottage.

"Here are the clothes, my lord," said the old man, laying his hand on the bundle.

"And here are mine," answered Lord Harry. "And the horse stands ready for you." With this he began to pull off the fine clothes in which he had had audience of the King, and he opened the bundle and put on the old and plain suit which it contained. Then he held out his hand to the old man, saying, "Give me the five crowns, Solomon, and our bargain is complete."

Then Solomon the Jew gave him five crowns and bade him farewell, and he placed the crowns in his purse and walked out of the cottage, possessing nothing in the world saving his old clothes, five crowns, and the golden pin that had fastened the ruddy hair of Princess Osra. For everything else that he had possessed, his lands and houses in

England, his horses and carriages, his money, his clothes, and all that was his, he had bartered with Solomon the Jew, in order that he might buy the ruby necklace which he had given to Princess Osra. Such was the strange madness wrought in him by her face.

It was now late evening, and he walked to and fro all night. In the morning he went to the shop of a barber and, in return for one of his crowns, the barber cropped his long curls short and shaved off his moustaches, and gave him a dye with which he stained his complexion to a darker tint; and he made his face dirty, and soiled his hands and roughened the skin of them by chafing them on some flints which lay by the roadside. Then, changing a second crown, he bought a loaf of bread, and set off to trudge to Strelsau, for in Strelsau was Osra, and he would not be anywhere else in the world. And when he had arrived there, he went to a sergeant of the King's Guard, and prevailed on him by a present of three crowns to enlist him as a trooper, and this the sergeant, having found that Lord Harry could ride, and knew how to use his sword, agreed to do. Thus Lord Harry became a trooper in the Guard of King Rudolf, having for all his possessions, save what the King's stores afforded him, a few pence and the golden pin that had fastened the hair of Princess Osra. But nobody knew him, except Solomon the Jew, and he, having made a good profit, held his peace, both then and afterwards.

Many a day Lord Harry mounted guard at the palace, and often he saw the King, with the Queen, ride out and back; but they did not notice the face of the trooper. Sometimes he saw the Princess also, but she did not look at him, although he could not restrain himself from looking at her; but since every man looked at her she had grown accustomed to being gazed at and took no heed of it. But once she wore the ruby necklace, and the breath of the trooper went quick and eager when he saw it on her neck; and a sudden flush of colour spread over all his face, so that the Princess, chancing to glance at him in passing, and seeing the colour beneath and through the dye that stained him, was greatly astonished, and she reined in her horse for an instant and looked very intently at him; yet she rode on again in silence.

That evening there came to the quarters of the King's Guard a waiting-woman, who asked to see the trooper who had mounted guard at the west gate of the palace that day; and when he came the woman held out to him a box of red morocco leather, saying, "It is for you."

But he answered, "It is not for me," and, turning away, left her. And this happened on three evenings. Then, on the fourth day, it was again his turn to mount guard at the palace; and when he had sat there on his horse for an hour, the Princess Osra rode out from under the portico; she rode alone and the ruby necklace was on her neck; and she said:

"I am going to ride outside the city by the river bank. Let a trooper follow me some way behind." And she signed with her hand to Lord Harry, and he rode after her through the streets, and out of the Western Gate; and they turned along the bank of the river. When they had gone three or four miles from the city, Osra halted, and beckoned to Lord Harry to approach her; and he came. But when she was about to speak to him and tell him that she knew him, a sudden new madness came on him; he seized her bridle, and dug his spurs deep into his horse's flanks, and the horse bounded forward at a gallop. In alarm the Princess cried out, but he did not heed her. Along the bank they galloped and when they met any one, which happened seldom (for the place was remote, and it was now evening), he bade her cover her face, and she obeyed, twisting her lace handkerchief about her face. Thus they rode till they came at nightfall to a bluff of rock high above the stream. Here Lord Harry suddenly checked the horses, flung himself from his saddle, and bade the Princess dismount. She obeyed, and stood facing him, pale with fear and apprehension, but wearing a proud and scornful air. And he cried:

"Is it not well you should die? For you live but to madden men and drive them to sin and folly."

"Nay," said she, "to men of good heart beauty leads to goodness. From yourself come the sin and folly, my lord;" and she laid hold of the ruby necklace and broke the clasp of it, and flung it on the ground before him. He took no heed of it, but seized her hand, and drew her to the edge of the bluff, saying:

"The world will be safer if I fling you down."

Then she looked in his face, and a sudden pity entered into her heart, and she said very gently:

"Sit down, my lord, and let me put my hands on your brow, for I think you are in a fever."

He sat down, all trembling and shaking like a man with ague, and she stripped off her gauntlets, and took his forehead between her hands; and he lay there quiet with his head between her hands. Presently his eyes closed, and he slept. But Osra did not know what to do, for darkness had fallen, and she dared not leave him alone there by the river. So she sat where she was, and in an hour, the night being fine and not cold, she grew weary; her hands fell away from his brow, and she sank back on the green turf, pillowing her head on a curved arm, and there she slept with the mad lord by her and the ruby necklace lying near them.

At midnight Lord Harry Culverhouse awoke, and saw Princess Osra sleeping peacefully, with a smile on her lips such as decks a child's in sleep. He rose and stood up on his feet, looking at her: and he heard nothing but the sound of the horses cropping the grass a little way off. Then he drew near her and gazed long on her face: and she opened her eyes and saw him; she smiled at him, and she said:

"Even here I am guarded by one of the gentlemen who guard me in the palace." And she closed her eyes again and turned to sleep.

A shiver ran through him. He dug his nails into the palms of his hands, and, turning, walked swiftly up and down on the bluff by the side of the river, while Osra slept.

Presently he fell on his knees beside her, beginning to murmur in a rapid rush of words: but he did not now curse her beauty, but blessed God for it, and blessed Him also for the preservation of his own honour. Thus he spent the night till day was near: then he bent over Osra, and looked once more on her: and he took up the ruby necklace and laid it lightly about her neck. Feeling the touch of it, cool and wet from the dew, she again opened her eyes, and, putting her knuckles in them, she rubbed gently; and she gasped a gentle yawn, saying: "Heigho, I am sleepy!" and sat up. And she said:

"Are you not sleepy, my lord?"

"I am on watch, madame," said Lord Harry Culverhouse.

As the Princess sat up, the ruby necklace fell from her neck into her lap. Seeing it, she held it up to him, saying:

"Take it again, and go to your own home. I am sure you gave too great a price for it."

He smiled, for she did not know how great the price was, and he asked:

"Must I, in my turn, give back the pin that fastened your hair?"

"No, keep the pin—it is worth nothing," she smiled. "Is it safe for me to go to sleep a little longer?"

"Who would harm you, madame? Even I have not harmed you."

"You!" said she, with a little laugh. "You would not harm me."

And she lay down again and closed her eyes.

Then Lord Harry Culverhouse sat down on the ground, resting his chin on his knees, and clasping his hands about his shins, and he cursed himself bitterly not now because he meditated any harm to her—for his hot fury was past, and he would have died before a hair of her head should be hurt but because of the evil that his wild and reckless madness had brought upon her. For he knew that soon there would be a pursuit, and that, if she and he were found there, it would become known who he was, and her fame would suffer injurious rumours by reason of what he had done. Therefore he made up his mind what he must next do, and he abandoned all the dreams that had led him into the foolish adventure on which he had embarked, and put from him the wickedness that had filled his heart when first he carried her to the bluff over the river. He rose on to his knees, and prayed that if his deed were a sin— for it seemed to him to be a necessary thing—then that it might be forgiven, but that, in any case, no hurt or harm should befall the Princess Osra by reason of anything that he had done. Finally he commended his soul to God. Then he took the ruby necklace in his hand and, holding it, walked to the edge of the bluff.

But at this instant the sound of the hoofs of a horse struck on his ear; the sound was loud and close, and he had no more time than to turn round before a horse was reined in suddenly by him, and a man leapt from it and ran at him and grappled with him. And Lord Harry perceived that the man was the King. For when Osra did not return, search parties had been sent out; the King himself headed one, and, having the best horse and being urged on by love and fear for his sister, he had outridden all the rest and had chanced to come alone where Osra and Lord Harry were; and he gripped Lord Harry furiously, cursing him for a scoundrel and demanding what he had done to the Princess. Then Lord Harry said:

"Do you not know me, sire? I am Harry Culverhouse."

Greatly astonished, the King loosed his hold and fell back a pace, for he could not understand what he heard, but yet knew the voice of his friend. Then, looking down, he beheld Osra sleeping peacefully as a child on the ground, with her cloak spread under her, that she might take no harm from the damp. But Lord Harry caught him by the arm, crying:

"Are there others coming after you?"

"Aye," said the King, "many others. The whole of the Guard are roused, and seek her high and low in the city and outside. But how came you here, man?"

Then Lord Harry told the King what he had done, speaking very briefly and hastily, but yet sparing nothing; and when he told him how he had carried off the Princess, the King's hand flew to the hilt of his sword. But Lord Harry said "Not yet," and continued to tell the King how Osra had pitied him, how he had watched by her, and how she had slept again, bidding him keep the pin. Then glancing at Osra, he lowered his voice and spoke very quick and urgently, and the King held out his hand and shook Lord Harry's hand, asking: "Is there no other way?" But Lord Harry shook his head; then he kissed the King's hand; next he went and kissed Osra's hand very softly, and looked for the last time on her face; and he drew the golden pin from his purse and he put it gently and deftly among her hair. Then taking the ruby necklace in his own hand and clenching it tight, he said to King Rudolf:

"Sire, there are some in the city that knew me before, but have not known me since I have been in your Guard, because I have altered my face. Take care that you so alter it that they do not know me again."

The King's breath caught in his throat, for he had loved Lord Harry Culverhouse, and he asked again:

"Is there no other way?"

"Hark!" said the other, "I hear the horses of your Guard drawing near; I hear them to east and west and north; and do you not see shapes riding there to the south, across the river? If I ride from here alive, I shall be taken, and the truth must be known. For my sake and hers, strike, sire."

The King took Lord Harry Culverhouse by the arm and drew him to him, saying:

"Must it be so, Harry? And we have lived as friends together!"

"The sound of the hoofs is very near, sire."

The King drew himself up to his height, and he raised his hat from his head, and bowed low to Lord Harry Culverhouse, and he said:

"Now praise be to God for the restoration of this gentleman to a sound mind, and may Christ grant him mercy for the sake of his honourable death!"

And he drew his sword from its sheath, and came up to Lord Harry Culverhouse, who stood on the edge of the bluff. The King raised his sword and struck with all his strength; the head split under the blow, and Lord Harry Culverhouse fell dead from the bluff into the river, holding the ruby necklace in his clenched hand. But the King shivered, and a short sob burst from him.

On this instant there arose an eager glad cry, and twenty of the Guard rushed forward, greeting the King and rejoiced to see the Princess. Roused by the noise of their coming, she sat up again, rubbing her eyes, and cried:

"Where is he? Where is Lord Harry?"

And she looked round on the troopers, and they gazed on her, much astonished at hearing what she said. But Rudolf came to her and took her hand, saying:

"Why, Osra, you have been dreaming! There is no Lord Harry here. Lord Harry Culverhouse is far off in his own country. Did that rascal of a trooper frighten you?"

Her eyes grew wide in wonder; but before she could speak he turned to the Guard, saying:

"By heaven's pleasure I came in time to prevent any harm, except the loss of a necklace my sister wore. For as I rode up, I saw a fellow stooping down by her and fumbling with the clasp of her necklace. He was one of your troop, and had ridden out behind her, and he must have carried her off by force: now he was endeavouring to rob her, and as I rode up to him he sprang away from her, holding her necklace in his hand: but I leapt down from my horse and ran at him, and he retreated in fear. Then I drew my sword, and drove him back to the edge of the bluff: and then I split his skull, and he fell into the river, still holding the necklace. But, thanks to God, the Princess is not hurt. Let search be made for the fellow's body, for perhaps the necklace will be still in his hand."

But one cried, "How came they here?"

"Ah, sister," said the King, fixing his eyes on Osra, "how came you here?"

Reading in the King's eyes the answer that he would have, she said:

"The trooper compelled me to come hither with him, and he threatened to kill me if I would not give him my necklace. But I refused: then he drew a knife and menaced me with it, and I fell into a swoon, and knew no more until I awoke and found you here; and now I see that my necklace is gone."

"Bring her horse," the King commanded, "and ride in front and behind. We will return to the city at the best speed we may."

Then he mounted the Princess on her horse, and rode by her side, supporting her with his arm: and the troopers were some way off in front and behind. But the Princess felt the pin again in her hair, and putting up her hand she pulled it out, and she said:

"He has given me back my pin."

"Of whom do you speak?" asked the King.

"Of Lord Harry Culverhouse. Is he indeed dead, Rudolf?"

"Are you indeed still dreaming?" answered the King with a laugh. "What had that fellow to do with Harry Culverhouse?"

"But the pin?" she cried.

"My wife set it in your hair, before you started, for she wished to replace the one you gave to Lord Harry,"

"She did not touch my hair to-day!" cried the Princess.

"Aye, but she did," said he.

The Princess suddenly fell to sobbing; and she said:

"Tell me the truth, tell me the truth. Surely it was in truth Lord Harry Culverhouse?"

Then Rudolf drew very close to her, and said softly:

"Sweet sister, the noble gentleman whom we knew, he whom I loved, and who loved you in chivalrous deference, went from us two months ago. Be not troubled about him, for now all is well with him. But there was an unhappy man with you, who was not our Harry Culverhouse, and who had murderous and mad thoughts in his heart. Yet at the end he also died as readily and as nobly as our dear friend himself would have died for your sake. I pray you ask no more of him, but be contented to know that though he died by the sword yet he died in peace and willingly. But of our dear friend, as we knew him, think as much as you will, for the love of an honest gentleman is a good thing to think of."

The Princess Osra, hearing this, laid her hand in her brother's hand, and for a long while she did not speak. Then she said:

"But our friend will not come again, Rudolf?"

"No, you will never see our friend again," answered the King.

"Then when you see him—for I think you will see him once again—lay this pin in his hand, and bid him take and keep it for the sake of the love I bear, him: perhaps he will hear you."

"It may be, I cannot tell," said the King.

"And if he has the necklace," said she, "pray him to give that to you, and sell it, Rudolf, and give the value of it in gifts to the poor. Yes, to all that are unhappy and afflicted, even as the poor man who was with me to-night."

"So be it, Osra," said the King, and he kissed her. But she burst again suddenly into passionate weeping, calling God to witness that her face was a curse to her and a curse to her friends, and praying the King to suffer her to take the veil in a convent, that she might trouble honest men no more. Thus he brought her in a sad plight to the palace, and gave her into the arms of his wife, still sobbing bitterly. And he himself took the pin, and when the body of the mad trooper was found, with his own hand he covered the face, and put the pin in the hand from which he took the ruby necklace and he sold the necklace, and used the proceeds of it as his sister had desired.

Thus the madness of Lord Harry Culverhouse, which was bred in him by the beauty of the Princess Osra, worked its way with him, and brought him first into peril of great villainy, and at last to death. And his name passed no more on the lips of any in Strelsau, nor between King Rudolf and his sister, while the story that the King had told to the troopers was believed by all, and none save the King knew what Lord Harry Culverhouse had done in his madness. But Osra mourned for him, and for a long while she would not go abroad, nor receive any of the princes or nobles who came to the Court, but lay still sick and full of grief, bewailing the harm that she had wrought. Yet, as time passed, she grew again happy, for she was young, and the world was sweet to her: and then, as King Rudolf had bidden her, she remembered Lord Harry Culverhouse as he had been before his madness came upon him. Yet still more did she remember how, even in his madness, he had done her no harm, but had watched beside her through the night, and had, as morning dawned, entreated death at the hands of the King, preferring to die rather than that the talk of a single idle tongue should fall foully on her name. Therefore she mourned for him with secret tears.

But he, although no monument marked his grave, and although men spoke only of the mad trooper who had robbed the Princess, yet slept soundly and at peace: and his right hand lay clenched upon his heart, and in it the golden pin that had fastened the ruddy hair of Princess Osra.

Chapter IV

The Courtesy of Christian the Highwayman

"I AM tired of men," cried Princess Osra, "and of suitors, and of princes. I will go to Zenda and ride in the forest all alone."

"You will meet men even there," said the King.

"How do you know that, sire?" she asked with a smile.

"At least I have found it impossible to avoid meeting women anywhere."

"I do not think it is the same thing," observed Osra smiling again.

The King said no more, but let her go her own way; and to Zenda she went, and rode in the forest all alone, meeting for many days no man at all, though, perhaps, she thought a little of those whom she had met, and (who can tell?) now and then of one whom she should some day meet. For the mind loves to entertain itself with such idle musings, and they are hardly conscious till a sudden smile or a beat of the heart betrays them to the abashed thinker. Just in this manner a flush had chanced to rise to Osra's cheek one day as she rode in a reverie, being above ten miles from the Castle and on the very edge of the kingdom's frontier, which skirts the extremity of the forest on the east. Breaking off her thoughts, half ashamed of them, she looked up and saw a very fine and powerful horse tethered to a tree a few yards away, saddled and bridled. Then she said to herself with a sigh, "Alas, here is a man as my brother said!" And she shook her head very sorrowfully.

The next instant she saw, as she had foreboded, a man approaching her; indeed, the matter was as bad as could be, for he was young and handsome, finely dressed, carrying a good sword by his side and a brace of pistols mounted in silver in his belt. He held a feathered hat in his hand, and, advancing with a deep bow, knelt on one knee by the Princess's horse, saying:

"Madame, if you will, you can do me a great service."

"If it be in my power, sir," she answered—for since fate compelled her to meet a man, she would not show him rudeness—"I am at your service."

"You see my horse there, madame? He is as dear as my life to me; and I fear I shall lose him, unless I have your aid," and he rose and stood looking at the Princess.

"Why, what threatens him?" she asked.

"I will tell you, madame. I come from across the frontier, from a secluded village nearly ten miles from here. There I live with my mother, whom I support. There is a rich fellow there, a farmer, Otho by name, who is, saving your presence, a plaguey boastful fellow. And he is to-day to be betrothed."

"Do you also love the lady?" asked Osra, thinking she had come at the cause of his trouble.

"Not I, madame. But this Otho boasted and vaunted so intolerably of her beauty, and of his own prowess and attraction, that last night I, led away by emulation (nay, I am ashamed to say that I had also drunk a flask of wine) wagered with him my horse against a thousand crowns— though the horse is worth two thousand—that I would bring with me to the feast a girl handsomer than his Lotta. But now it is eleven o'clock, and the feast is at one o'clock, and I have no girl to show, ugly or handsome. And if I lose my horse I must hang myself, for I cannot live without him."

"You cannot live without your horse?" she asked in surprise.

"At least, madame," he answered in some confusion, "his loss would go near to breaking my heart."

"But is this Lotta so handsome that you can find none to surpass her?"

"She is, indeed, wonderfully handsome. In the village they call her the most beautiful girl in the world."

"Then, sir, it seems to me that your wager was most improvident and rash. For you are certain to lose it."

"Alas, yes!" he answered in great distress. "I am certain to lose; for there are, I think, only two ladies in the world who could save me, and one would not."

"Two ladies? Who are they?"

"MADAME, IF YOU WILL,
YOU CAN DO ME A GREAT SERVICE."

"Madame," said he, "before you came in sight, I sat desolate and despairing on the ground, and what I said to myself was, 'If what men say is true, there is only one lady who could save me. But how shall I, poor Christian Hantz, come at the Princess Osra? And would she put on a country girl's dress and go to the feast with me? Alas, it is impossible! And there is no other lady in the world beautiful enough.' But then—"

"Well, sir, what then?" asked Osra, playing with her whip and smothering a smile.

"Then, madame," said Christian, "I looked up and I saw you, and I cried, 'A fig for the Princess Osra! For here is a lady more beautiful than all they tell of Princess Osra; I will throw myself at her feet and pray her in pity to help me.'"

Still Osra hid her smile, and so busy was she with this task that she did not perceive that Christian also hid a smile; but she thought that he did not know her, whereas he had seen her several times, and had this day tracked her in the forest, knowing that she was accustomed to ride there.

"But where," she asked, "would the lady who went with you get the dress you speak of?"

"At my mother's cottage, madame, where my mother would wait on her."

"And when could she be back at this spot?"

"By five in the afternoon, madame. I would myself escort her."

"And why, sir, should she rescue you from the straits into which your folly has led you?"

"Alas, madame, for no reason, unless, by a divine miracle, she should prove as kind as she is beautiful."

"You have a rash tongue, sir, in other matters than the making of wagers."

And she looked at him. For she was very sorely tempted to do what he prayed of her; and she said:

"Has the Princess Osra ever ridden through your village?"

"Never, madame."

"But some there may know her face, and then they will think nothing of mine."

"It is unlikely that any one there should have seen even a picture of her, for they are quiet folk and do not go abroad."

"Besides, in a peasant's dress—" began Osra meditatively. But she stopped, blushing and laughing. And Christian caught her hand and kissed it, crying:

"For heaven's sake, come, madame!"

He was so earnest, and his earnestness so became his bronzed face and bright eyes, that Osra could not deny him, but she swore him to secrecy, and agreed to ride with him, blaming herself all the while very greatly, and blaming yet more that Fate which would not allow her to be quit of the troublesome race of men even in the recesses of the forest of Zenda.

Turning their horses, therefore, towards the frontier, they set them at a smart canter, for there was little time to lose if they were to come to the feast by one o'clock; and shortly before noon, having struck a bye-path through the trees, they came on a small cottage that stood apart and by itself; and a hill rose from it.

"On the other side of the hill lies the village, madame," said Christian, jumping from his horse. "And this is my cottage. Hallo, there, mother!"

An old woman came out, neatly and cleanly clad. Christian ran up to her, spoke to her briefly, and brought her to Osra. The worthy dame, bewildered by the appearance and stately air of the Princess, did nothing but curtsey and murmur incoherent thanks, but Osra, now caught by the excitement of the enterprise, clapped her hands, crying:

"Quick, quick, or we shall be too late!"

So Christian lifted her down and led away the horses to a shed behind the cottage. But the old woman led Osra in, and took her to the bedroom, where lay a dress such as the peasant girls wore. Osra took up the skirt, and looked at it curiously.

"Must I indeed wear this?" she asked. "And I am somewhat tall, mother!"

The old woman said that nothing would serve save the dress, and Osra sighed. Yet as there was no help for it, she suffered the old woman to help her in getting it on.

So the door was shut, and Christian sat smiling in the sun outside, well pleased at the success of his audacious scheme, and feeling Otho's crowns already in his pocket.

Still less did he doubt of this most desirable result when the door of the cottage again opened and Osra came out, blushing, and yet biting her lips to keep back her laughter. Her hair was plaited in two long plaits; she wore a white bodice, and over it a jacket of black velvet, and a red skirt hung full from her waist to but a very little below her knee;

then came hose of red also—for it was a holiday, and the best of all was
worn—and stout square-toed shoes. Osra in her heart loved all except
the shoes, yet she declared that she loathed all except the shoes. And
Christian, with eyes cast most demurely on the ground, prayed her to
forgive the sad necessity, yet assured her that Lotta would die of envy
that very day.

"Let us go then," said Osra. "For the sooner we go, the sooner will it
be done and I can get rid of these ridiculous clothes. Heaven have
mercy on me and grant that I may meet none who know me!"

They were mounting the hill now, the old woman standing at the
cottage door and watching. When they reached the top Osra saw a
small village nestling in the valley below, and the sound of music struck
on her ear. At this a sudden fear seized her, and putting out her hand
she caught Christian by the sleeve, saying:

"Will they know me?"

"Not they, madame," said he. But as he spoke his eyes fell on a ring
that the Princess wore, a gem engraved with the Royal Arms. "Not
they, if you conceal that ring;" and for a moment he looked in her face,
and he smiled.

Osra uttered a little cry, as she hastily plucked the ring from her
finger, and gave it to him, saying:

"Keep it safe, and do not forget to give it me again."

But she would not meet his glance, for she began from now to suspect
that he knew who she was.

The sound of music came from a solid square-built house that stood
on the outskirts of the village, and coming nearer they saw a long table
spread in the shade near the house, and a company of men and women
seated at it. The Princess was somewhat comforted to find that the
girls' dresses were in all respects like her own, though hers seemed
newer and more handsome; therefore she took courage, and put her
arm inside Christian's arm, saying:

"Since I have accepted the part, I will play it. Come, sir, let us go
and challenge Lotta. Your horse is at stake!"

"He is in no danger," said Christian, "and I am worth a thousand
crowns." And his eyes most plainly added the reason which led him to
these comfortable conclusions.

Now at this moment Otho, having toasted the company and accepted
their good wishes, was standing up before them all, Lotta standing by
him, her hand in his; and he vowed (as was but right) all manner of

love and devotion to her, and declared that she was the prettiest girl in the world; in truth she was very pretty, being, although low of stature, most admirably formed, having golden hair, the pinkest of cheeks and large blue eyes that followed a man about in a most appealing and distracting manner. So that Otho had good reason to be content, and would have come to no harm, had it not been for that old extravagance of lovers which will not allow this world to hold more than one pretty girl—the truth being, of course, quite otherwise. But, led on by this infatuation, Otho cried:

"I dare any man to find so pretty a girl! As for Master Christian whose wager you heard—why, this evening his fine horse shall feed in my stable!"

"Softly, friend Otho, softly," came to the ears of the feasters from behind the trees. "Mistress Lotta is very pretty, but I have here a girl whom some think handsome. Well, this worthy company shall judge." And Christian came from the shelter of the trees leading Osra by the hand, and he set her opposite to Lotta, where all could see her. And all looked and beheld her with amazement. But none spoke. So they rested for a long while, Christian smiling and Osra's eyes being set on Lotta, while Otho did nothing but gaze at Osra.

Presently a low murmur began to run along the table. "Who is she?" asked some one, but none could answer. "Who is she?" called an old man to Christian, but he answered, "What's that to you? Is she not fairer?" And when the others asked whence she came, he made the same answer.

But one young fellow leant from his place and plucked Christian's sleeve, saying, "Is she promised to you?" and at this Christian frowned, answering, "At least she is not for you," while Osra, overhearing, blushed mightily. Then Otho, still saying nothing, suddenly lugged out a great purse of money, and flung it violently into the middle of the table with a curse, and Christian with a mocking lift of his hat, came forward, and, taking it, tossed it up and down in his hand, crying, "Is it fair weight, neighbour Otho?" Otho did not heed him, but turned suddenly to Lotta and put his arm round her waist, saying:

"Aye, it is true. The devil must have sent her, but it is true. Yet you are pretty too, my lass." For Lotta, after looking at all the company and at Osra, had been so sorely wounded in her pride and robbed of her triumph, that, poor child, she had begun to weep, hiding her face in her hands, and Otho was trying to comfort her, though, lover as he was, he could not for the life of him declare that she was more beautiful than the girl whom Christian had brought. And they all moved from their places and came to stand round Osra. But she, after a moment, caught from Christian the bag that he tossed so exultantly, crying to him: "I'll be your debtor for it;" and bursting through the ring, she ran round the table and came to Lotta, and, pulling the girl's hands down from her face, she thrust the bag into her hands, and began to talk to her, whispering low, and looking into her frightened eyes with shining eyes.

"Ah, my dear," said Osra, "see, he still loves you, dear. Ah, why did I come? But I am going away, yes, now, and I shall never come here again. I do harm wherever I go! Yes, but you'll be the prettiest girl in the village always! Otho, Otho, kiss her, Otho! Tell her that you love her, Otho. Don't stand there dumb. Oh, how stupid men are! Don't you see what she wants? Yes, do it again. I never saw anybody so pretty, Otho. Yes, yes, dear, keep the bag. It's from me; you must keep it, and buy pretty clothes and be prettier than ever, for Otho's sake, because he loves you."

By the time the Princess Osra had ended her consolations, behold she was very nearly crying herself! But Lotta put her arms round the Princess's neck and kissed her, because she said that Otho still loved her; and in her gratitude for this, she forgot thanks for the bag of crowns, or even to wonder who this girl was that could give away a thousand crowns. But in this the rest of the company were not like her, and an eager murmuring marked the excitement with which they watched the scene; and they cried to Christian:

"Look after your crowns," and thought him mad when he shook his head jauntily, answering:

"Let Otho do what he will with them."

Then, their interest growing more and more intense, they crowded round the Princess, scanning her very closely; and she was in great fear that she would be known, and also in some embarrassment from the ardent glances and free comments of the simple countrymen, who were accustomed to say what they thought with more plainness than were the gentlemen of the Court. So that at length, fairly alarmed, she gave Lotta a last hasty kiss, and made her way to Christian, crying:

"Take me away."

"Aye, madame," said he, and he put her arm in his and turned away. But all the company followed him, staring and gossiping and crowding, so that Lotta and Otho were left alone at the feast which Otho had provided, with nothing to console them but one another's love and the happily recovered thousand crowns. And the crowd pressed hard on Osra and Christian, being full of eagerness to see where the girl went and what became of her. Thus they reached the top of the hill and came in sight of Christian's cottage. But now Christian suddenly loosed Osra's arm and, turning round, faced the throng of inquisitive folk; with either hand he drew a silver-mounted pistol from his belt; and when he had cocked the pair, he pointed them at his friends and neighbours, saying in a quiet and pleasant voice: "I shall count to twenty. Any one who means to be within range when I come to twenty had best now order his coffin."

At this a great grumbling arose among them; yet they knew Christian, and did not wait till he had counted, but one and all turned tail and ran down the hill much quicker than they had come up. But one or two fellows, resentful and malicious because of their disappointment, as soon as they found themselves out of range, turned round and shouted:

"Aye, he is ready with his pistol, is Christian. We know him. Highwayman! Whom did you last rob?" And Christian went red as the frock that Osra wore. But she turned questioning eyes on him.

"Yes," said he sullenly. "They say highwayman; it is true. I am a robber. That is why I said, madame, that I could not live without my horse."

"Come," said Osra, "let us go to the cottage."

So they returned together to the cottage, saying nothing. There Osra put on her own clothes again, and having bidden farewell to the old woman who asked no questions of her, mounted her horse. Then Christian said:

"Shall I ride with you, madame?"

She bowed her head in assent.

Till they entered the forest the Princess did not speak. But then she sighed, saying:

"I am sorry that I went with you. For if you had lost your horse maybe you would have ceased from your way of life. It is better to lose a horse than to be hanged."

"Madame," said he, "you speak prudently. Yet I had rather be hanged than lose him."

"I am in your debt a thousand crowns," said she, and, stopping her horse, she wrote for him an order for a thousand crowns, and she signed it with her own name, Osra, and gave it to him. He received it bowing very low.

WITH EITHER HAND HE DREW A SILVER-MOUNTED PISTOL.

"You knew me all the time?" she asked.

"Yes, madame," said he. They had now come to where he had first met her.

"Why do you live by robbery?" she asked.

"For the love of the same thing that made you come with me to-day, madame."

"But could you not find what you love in the King's service?"

"I do not like service, madame," said Christian. "I love to be free."

She paused for a moment, and then said in a lower tone:

"Could you not endure my service, sir?"

"In that I shall now live and die, madame," said he, and she felt his eyes upon her.

Again in silence they rode on; it was evening now, and had grown dark, and presently the lantern in the tower of the keep of Zenda became visible. Then Osra drew rein.

"For my sake," said she, "rob no more."

"What you command, madame, is my law. And here is your ring."

"Keep the ring," she said. "But when I can serve you, you shall send it back to me, and ask what you will in return for it."

"There is nothing," said he, very low, and looking away from her, "that I would take in exchange for it."

"A foolish man or only a foolish speech?" she asked as lightly as she could, with one fleeting glance at his face.

"A foolish man, madame, it may be, but a true speech," and he bent bareheaded in his saddle and raised her hand to his lips. And, still bareheaded, he turned away and rode back at a canter into the forest. But the Princess Osra rode on to the Castle, wondering greatly at what she had done that day.

Yet she could not be very sorry that she had saved his horse for him, and she trusted that Otho and Lotta would be happy, and she thought that one man was, after all, as good flesh and blood as another, and then that she was a Princess and he a robber, and that his eyes had been over bold. Yet there was deference in them also.

"It is a great pity that he should be a robber," sighed the Princess, as she reached the Castle.

The Princess Osra's carriage was within two miles of Strelsau when she put her head out of the window and asked the officer who rode by the wheel why such a throng of people hastened to the city.

"It is nothing, madame," answered he, saluting. "It is only that two rogues are to be hanged to-day."

"What pleasure is there in seeing men hanged?" asked Osra scornfully. "I wish I had not come to-day." And she drew her head back in disgust. Then she called:

"Go slowly, and do not let me get into the middle of the wild beasts who go to gloat over men being hanged."

So the horses were checked to a walk, and thus the carriage proceeded slowly towards Strelsau. But presently the Princess put her head out of the window again and asked:

"Who are to be hanged to-day, sir?"

"The noted highwayman, Sigismund Kohl, madame," said the officer. "He robbed the Archbishop's coach in the forest of Zenda; but they pursued him over the frontier and tracked him to the cottage of the other rogue, who had a part in many previous robberies, though not in this. The second fellow hid Kohl, and tried to put off the officers, but they caught them both, and both are to be hanged."

"It seems hard," said Osra, "to hang the one who only sheltered his friend. He could do no less."

"Nay, madame, he richly deserves it. Besides his previous robberies, he is gravely suspected of a most foul murder. For a few weeks ago he was in company with a girl, and she seemed to have money and to spare, and was mighty pretty too, they say. Now he can give no account of what has become of her; but they have found all the clothes she wore hidden away in his house, and he says his mother bought the clothes. But they are a girl's clothes, not an old woman's. It looks black; but luckily the other matter is enough to hang him on. His mother's clothes, in faith! Would an old woman, who died three weeks ago, have bought a new red frock and smart red stockings for herself?"

"A red frock? Red stockings? And the mother is dead? Dead of what?"

"Of a chill, madame, such as carries old people off suddenly. Yes, it looks black, and so the people think, for when the pair were brought into the city, though the rascals cheered Kohl who had only robbed the Archbishop, they pelted and came near to killing Christian Hantz."

The Princess's face went pale, and she sank back, murmuring "Christian Hantz!" But in another moment she cried:

"At what hour is the hanging?"

"At noon, madame; that is, half an hour from now."

SHE ASKED THE OFFICER WHY A THRONG OF PEOPLE HASTENED TO THE CITY.

Then the Princess cried in a loud urgent tone:

"Faster, faster! Drive at top speed!" The officers looked at her in wonder; but she cried: "A hundred crowns to the coachman if he brings me to the place before noon! Quick, quick!" For she was all on fire at the thought that Christian Hantz was to be hanged, not for any new robbery but because he had sheltered his friend. And she knew how the red skirt and the red stockings came in his house; her breath caught in her throat, as she thought how he had suffered stoning and execration rather than betray her secret. And she cried out to herself as she was carried along, "But the ring! Why did he not send the ring?"

By now they were at the gates of the city, and now within them. The officer and the two men who were with him rode forward to clear the road for the Princess. Thus they made their way on, until they came to the street which leads from the West Gate to the Cathedral, and could see the gibbet that had been raised before the prison, between the Cathedral and the Palace. But here the whole street was blocked with people, and the officer could not get the carriage through, for the folk were thick as swarming bees all across the roadway, and even if they would have moved, they could not; so the carriage came to a dead stand, while the officer said to Princess Osra:

"Madame, it is useless, we cannot get through them." Osra sprang from the carriage, and she said:

"You have two men with you, sir. For God's sake, gentlemen, bring me through to the foot of the scaffold. I care not if it costs me my life."

"Nor we, madame, though it costs us ours, since it is your pleasure," they said, as every man in the city would have said for the Princess Osra. And the two men went ahead, while Osra followed with the officer; and pushing and struggling, and dodging in and out, aye, and when need was, hitting, and buffeting, and kicking, the three took her through into the square of the Cathedral. And the clock in the great tower struck noon.

As the bell boomed a cry went up from the thronged square; the body of a man shot from the scaffold to the top of the gibbet and hung there. The people cried aloud, some cheering, some also groaning and weeping.

"Who is it, who is it?" asked the Princess.

"It is Sigismund Kohl, madame," said the officer.

"Then on, on, on!" she commanded, and again they struggled forward. Now a louder and fiercer cry rang out as a man was brought forward on the scaffold, in his shirt and breeches. A priest was with him, holding a crucifix before his eyes. King Rudolf, who sat at a window of his palace, asked why they delayed to string the rascal up; and one of his gentlemen answered:

"Sire, the priest begged a few minutes' delay. For the obstinate rogue will not confess to the murder of the girl, and therefore cannot receive absolution, and the priest is loth to have him hanged without it."

"He shall be hanged without it, unless his conscience act quickly," said the King. But a moment later, he asked:

"What is the tumult in the corner of the square? There is a fight there. Let it be seen to."

Indeed there was a fight; for the three with Osra were bent on getting through, and the crowd would not let them through; and they struck at the crowd, and the crowd at them. But suddenly some one, peering past the Guards, exclaimed: "The Princess Osra, the Princess!" Then the blows ceased, and the crowd began slowly to give back, making way for Osra. And she walked between walls of people, yet did not seem to see or to take heed of any of them; her eyes were glued to the man on the scaffold. For even now the priest, who had held the crucifix, turned sorrowfully away, and signed with his hand to the hangman.

Again the people shouted fiercely for Christian's death; and he, stepping forward, gave himself into the executioner's hands. Those who were near him saw that there was a smile on his lips, and, as the hangman took hold of him, he kissed a little packet which he held in his right hand. But the people shrieked loudly: "Murderer, murderer! Where is the girl?" At this, stung beyond endurance, Christian cried, so loudly that his voice rose above the clamour:

"I am no murderer, I did not touch a hair of her head."

"Then where is she, where is she?" they shouted.

"I do not know," said he; and he added in a low tone, kissing his little packet again.

"Wherever she is, God in his graciousness send her joy." And he turned to the executioner, saying, "Get on, man." But then he looked as it were for the last time on the living sea of faces round him, and suddenly, out of all of them, he saw one.

What Christian saw the King saw also, and he rose from his chair with an oath and a laugh.

"This sister of mine is a wonderful wench," said he. "Come, let us see why she will not have this rascal hanged. Run, some one, and tell them not to string him up till I give the word."

The King walked out of the palace and came into the square, the Guard parting the people before him; and Osra, seeing him coming, stood now quite still, blushing and smiling, although she was very ashamed and panted sorely.

Then the King came and faced her, saying nothing, but lifting his eyebrows and smiling whimsically; but at last he whispered:

"What, was there a man in the forest, Osra?"

And she answered: "Do not ask me that, sire, but ask Christian Hantz what is in the packet which he kissed as the hangman took hold of him."

"He is not only a robber, but a murderer also, though he will not own to it."

"No, he is no murderer," said she. "Look in the packet."

"Then come and look with me," said the King, and taking her hand he led her up on to the scaffold in the sight of all the people, who wondered and laughed; for they always laughed at the ways of the Princess Osra. But she flew straight across to Christian, who fell on one knee with the rope round his neck.

"Give me the packet," she cried, and she tore it open. And in it she found her order for a thousand crowns and the gem engraved with the Royal Arms. For an instant she looked at Christian, and then she said:

"You have not got money for the order? Yet my name is good for a thousand crowns."

"To me, madame, it was better than fifty thousand."

"But," she broke out eagerly; "you should have sent the ring. I could have saved you."

"But you would have kept it in return for the service, madame."

"Aye, sir, that was the bargain," said Osra, with a little low laugh.

"I knew it. And I preferred to die with it rather than live without it."

"Another foolish speech!"

"Yes, for the man is foolish, madame."

"And they cry to you, 'Where is the girl?' And you do not answer, but die under a foul charge!"

To this Christian Hantz made no answer at all, unless it were one to murmur mournfully:

"And, madame, they have taken from me the red skirt and—"

The Princess Osra suddenly turned from him, and went to the King, who had stood regarding her; and she knelt down before him, saying:

"Sire and dear brother, pardon this man. He did but shelter his friend, and he will rob no more."

"I might forgive him his robberies, if he would take service in my army."

"Yes, in my regiment of Guards!" she cried.

"But how shall I forgive that foul murder, of which he is certainly guilty? For where, sister, is the pretty girl, of whom no traces can be found saving her dress, her red skirt, and—?"

"Sire, these things—I pray you sire, let your gentlemen stand back a little."

"Stand back, then, gentlemen," said the King.

"These things, sire, were, by a strange chance, in the little parcel that the poor man kissed. Though why he kissed it, I do not know."

The King took Osra's order for a thousand crowns, and also the gem engraved with the Royal Arms; he looked at them and at his sister.

"Therefore, sire," said she, "I ask life and pardon for the most courteous gentleman in your dominions. For he prized my ring above his life and my secret above his honour. Sire, such men should live and not die."

The King turned to his officers, and said:

"Gentlemen, the Princess knows that the girl is alive and well and has no complaint against this man. For he might not in honour tell who or where she was. And. for the rest, he did but shelter his friend, and my sister is surety that he will rob no more. May he live?"

When they heard this, they all declared that Christian should live, and they went into the crowd and told the people that the girl was found. Then the people suddenly veered round and began to cheer Christian, and some cried, "Who is the girl?" and laughed merrily, conceiving that it was a love affair on which Christian had been engaged; and because he preferred to die under an imputation of murder rather than endanger his love's reputation, he became a hero with them; and when they heard he was not to die, they dispersed in the utmost good temper, cheering him and the King and above all the Princess Osra, whom they loved.

But she went again to Christian, and bade the hangman take the rope off his neck.

"Will you serve in my regiment of Guards, sir?" she asked. "Or is service still irksome to you?"

"I will serve you, madame," said Christian.

"And since you will need equipment, get money for this order," and she gave him again the order.

"I must needs obey you, madame, though reluctantly."

"It is well, sir. I trust you will serve me faithfully. I bid you farewell, sir," and she bowed slightly, and turned as if to leave him. And he said nothing, but stood looking at her, so that presently she blushed, saying:

"They will let you have those things now, sir."

Christian bowed very low, and, raising himself again, looked at her ring.

"Nay, I cannot do that," said Princess Osra. "But you will see it now and then, and, now and then, maybe, you can touch it." And she put the ring on her finger and held out her hand to him. He knelt and kissed the ring and then her hand; but he looked very glum. And the Princess laughed openly at him, her eyes dancing in delight and amusement. But he still looked more as though he were going to be hanged than he had any time before in the day. So that the King, pointing at him, said to Osra:

"An ungrateful dog! Upon my soul he looks as though he were sorry not to be hanged! Do you call that courtesy?"

But the Princess laughed softly, and rubbed the ring on her finger, as she answered:

"Aye, sire, I call that the best of courtesy."

CHAPTER V

The Sin of the Bishop of Modenstein

IN the days of Rudolf III there stood on the hill opposite the Castle of Zenda, and on the other side of the valley in which the town lies, on the site where the *château* of Tarlenheim now is situated, a fine and strong castle belonging to Count Nikolas of Festenburg. He was a noble of very old and high family, and had great estates; his house being, indeed, second only to the Royal House in rank and reputation. He himself was a young man of great accomplishments, of a domineering temper, and of much ambition; and he had gained distinction in the wars that marked the closing years of the reign of King Henry the Lion. With King Rudolf he was not on terms of cordial friendship, for he despised the King's easy manners and carelessness of dignity, while the King had no love for a gentleman whose one object seemed to be to surpass and outshine him in the eyes of his people, and who never rested from extending and fortifying his castle until it threatened to surpass Zenda itself both in strength and magnificence. Moreover Nikolas, although maintaining a state ample and suitable to his rank, was yet careful and prudent, while Rudolf spent all that he received and more besides, so that the Count grew richer and the King poorer. But in spite of these causes of difference, the Count was received at Court with apparent graciousness, and no open outburst of enmity had yet occurred, the pair being, on the contrary, often together, and sharing their sports and pastimes with one another.

Now most of these diversions were harmless, or, indeed, becoming and proper, but there was one among them full of danger to a man of hot head and ungoverned impulse such as King Rudolf was. And this

one was diceing, in which the King took great delight, and in which
the Count Nikolas was very ready to encourage him. The King, who
was generous and hated to win from poor men or those who might be
playing beyond their means in order to give him pleasure, was delighted
to find an opponent whose purse was as long or longer than his own,
and thus gradually came to pass many evenings with the boxes in
Nikolas's company. And the more evenings he passed the deeper he
fell into the Count's debt; for the King drank wine, while the Count
was content with small beer, and when the King was losing he doubled
his stakes, whereas the Count took in sail if the wind seemed adverse.
Thus always and steadily the debt grew, till at last Rudolf dared not
reckon how large it had become, nor did he dare to disclose it to his
advisers. For there were great public burdens already imposed by reason
of King Henry's wars, and the citizens of Strelsau were not in a mood
to bear fresh exaction, nor to give their hard earnings for the payment
of the King's gambling debts; in fine although they loved the Elphbergs
well enough, they loved their money more. Thus the King had no
resource except in his private possessions, and these were of no great
value, saving the Castle and estate of Zenda.

At length, when they had sat late one night and the throws had
gone all the evening against the King and for Nikolas, the King flung
himself back in his chair, drained his glass, and said impatiently:

"I am weary of the game! Come, my lord, let us end it."

"I would not urge you, sire, a moment beyond what you desire. I
play but for your pleasure."

"Then my pleasure has been your profit," said the King with a vexed
laugh, "for I believe I am stripped of my last crown. What is my debt?"

The Count, who had the whole sum reckoned on his tablets took
them out, and shewed the King the amount of the debt.

"I cannot pay it," said Rudolf. "I would play you again, to double
the debt or wipe it out, but I have nothing of value enough to stake."

The desire which had been nursed for long in the Count's heart
now saw the moment of its possible realisation.

He leant over the table, and, smoothing his beard with his hand,
said gently:

"The amount is no more than half the value of your Majesty's Castle
and demesne of Zenda."

The King started and forced a laugh.

"Aye, Zenda spoils the prospect from Festenburg, does it?" said he.

"But I will not risk Zenda. An Elphberg without Zenda would seem like a man robbed of his wife. We have had it since we have had anything or been anything. I should not seem King without it."

"As you will, sire. Then the debt stands?" He looked full and keenly into the King's eyes, asking without words, "How will you pay it?" and adding without words, "Paid it must be." And the King read the unspoken words in the eyes of Count Nikolas.

The King took up his glass, but finding it empty flung it angrily on the floor, where it shivered into fragments at Count Nikolas's feet; and he shifted in his chair and cursed softly under his breath. Nikolas sat with the dice-box in his hand and a smile on his lips; for he knew that the King could not pay, and therefore must play, and he was in the vein, and did not doubt of winning from the King Zenda and its demesne. Then he would be the greatest lord in the kingdom, and hold for his own a kingdom within the kingdom, and the two strongest places in all the land. And a greater prize might then dangle in reach of his grasp.

"The devil spurs and I gallop," said the King at last. And he took up the dice-box and rattled it.

"Fortune will smile on you this time, sire, and I shall not grieve at it," said Count Nikolas with a courteous smile.

"Curses on her!" cried the King. "Come, my lord, a quick ending to it! One throw, and I am a free man, or you are master of my castle."

"One throw let it be, sire, for it grows late," assented Nikolas with a careless air; and they both raised the boxes and rattled the dice inside them. The King threw; his throw was a six and a five, and a sudden gleam of hope lit up his eyes; he leant forward in his chair, gripping the elbows of it with his hands; his cheeks flushed and his breath came quickly. With a bow Count Nikolas raised his hand and threw. The dice fell and rolled on the table. The King sank back; and the Count said with a smile of apology and a shrug of his shoulders:

"Indeed I am ashamed. For I cannot be denied to-night."

For Count Nikolas of Festenburg had thrown sixes, and thereby won from the King the Castle and demesne of Zenda.

He rose from his chair, and, having buckled on his sword that had lain on the table by him, and taking his hat in his hand, stood looking down on the King with a malicious smile on his face. And he said with a look that had more mockery than respect in it:

"Have I your Majesty's leave to withdraw? For ere day dawn, I have matters to transact in Strelsau, and I would be at my Castle of Zenda to-night."

Then King Rudolf took a sheet of paper and wrote an order that the Castle, and all that was in it, and all the demesne should be surrendered to Count Nikolas of Festenburg on his demand, and he gave the paper to Nikolas. Then he rose up and held out his hand, which Nikolas kissed, smiling covertly, and the King said with grace and dignity:

"Cousin, my Castle has found a more worthy master. God give you joy of it."

And he motioned with his hand to be left alone. Then, when the Count had gone, he sat down in his chair again, and remained there till it was full day, neither moving nor yet sleeping. There he was found by his gentlemen when they came to dress him, but none asked him what had passed.

Count Nikolas, now Lord of Zenda, did not so waste time, and the matters that he had spoken of did not keep him long in Strelsau; but in the early morning he rode out, the paper which the King had written in his belt.

First he rode with all speed to his own house of Festenburg, and there he gathered together all his followers, servants, foresters, and armed retainers, and he told them that they were to ride with him to Zenda, for that Zenda was now his and not the King's. At this they were greatly astonished, but they ate the fine dinner and drank the wine which he provided, and in the evening they rode down the hill very merry, and trotted, nearly a hundred strong, through the town, making a great noise, so that they disturbed the Bishop of Modenstein, who was lying that night at the inn in the course of a journey from his See to the Capital; but nobody could tell the Bishop why they rode to Zenda, and presently the Bishop, being wearied with travelling, went to his bed.

Now King Rudolf, in his chagrin and dismay, had himself forgotten, or had at least neglected to warn the Count of Festenburg, that his sister Princess Osra was residing at the Castle of Zenda; for it was her favourite resort, and she often retired from the Court and spent many days there alone. There she was now with two of her ladies, a small retinue of servants, and no more than half a dozen Guards; and when Count Nikolas came to the gate, it being then after nine, she had gone to her own chamber, and sat before the mirror, dressed in a loose white gown, with her ruddy hair unbound and floating over her shoulders. She was reading an old story book, containing tales of Helen of Troy, of Cleopatra, of Berenice, and other lovely ladies, very elegantly related and embellished with fine pictures. And the Princess, being very much absorbed in the stories, did not hear nor notice the arrival of the Count's company, but continued to read, while Nikolas roused the watchmen, and the bridge was let down, and the steward summoned. Then Nikolas took the steward aside, and skewed him the King's order, bearing the King's seal, and the steward, although both greatly astonished and greatly grieved, could not deny the letter or the seal, but declared himself ready to obey and to surrender the Castle; and the sergeant in command of the Guard said the same; but, they added, since the Princess was in the Castle, they must inform her of the matter, and take her commands.

"Aye, do," said Nikolas, sitting down in the great hall. "Tell her not to be disturbed, but to give me the honour of being her host for as long as she will, and say that I will wait on her, if it be her pleasure."

But he smiled to think of the anger and scorn with which Osra would receive the tidings when the steward delivered them to her.

In this respect the event did not fall short of his expectations, for she was so indignant and aghast that, thinking of nothing but the tidings, she flung away the book and cried: "Send the Count here to me," and stood waiting for him there in her chamber, in her white gown and with her hair unbound and flowing down over her shoulders. And when he came she cried: "What is this, my lord?" and listened to his story with parted lips and flashing eyes, and thus read the King's letter and saw the King's seal. And her eyes filled with tears, but she dashed them away with her hand. Then the Count said, bowing to her as mockingly as he had bowed to her brother:

"It is the fortune of the dice, madame."

"Yes, my lord, as you play the game," said she.

His eyes were fixed on her, and it seemed to him that she was more beautiful in her white gown and with her hair unbound over her shoulders, than he had ever felt her to be before, and he eyed her closely. Suddenly she looked at him, and for a moment he averted his eyes; but he looked again and her eyes met his. For several moments she stood rigid and motionless. Then she said:

"My lord, the King has lost the Castle of Zenda, which is the home and cradle of our House. It was scarcely the King's alone to lose. Have I no title in it?"

"It was the King's, madame, and now it is mine," smiled Nikolas.

"Well, then, it is yours," said she, and taking a step towards him, she said: "Have you a mind to venture it again, my lord?"

"I would venture it only against a great stake," said he, smiling still, while his eyes were fixed on her face and marked every change in the colour of her cheeks.

"I can play dice as well as the King," she cried. "Are we not all gamblers, we Elphbergs?" And she laughed bitterly.

"But what would your stake be?" he asked sneeringly.

Princess Osra's face was now very pale, but her voice did not tremble and she did not flinch; for the honour of her House and of the throne was as sacred to her as her salvation, and more than her happiness.

"A stake, my lord," said she, "that many gentlemen have thought above any castle in preciousness."

"Of what do you speak?" he asked, and his voice quivered a little, as a man's does in excitement. "For pardon me, madame, but what have you of such value?"

"I have what the poorest girl has and it is of the value that it pleased God to make it and pleases men to think it," said Osra. "And all of it I will stake against the King's Castle of Zenda and its demesne."

Count Nikolas's eyes flashed and he drew nearer to her; he took his dice-box from his pocket, and he held it up before her, and he whispered in an eager hoarse voice:

"Name this great stake, madame; what is it?"

"It is myself, my lord," said Princess Osra.

"Yourself?" he cried wondering, though he had half guessed.

"Aye. To be the Lord of Zenda is much. Is it not more to be husband to the King's sister?"

"It is more," said he, "when the King's sister is the Princess Osra." And he looked at her now with open admiration. But she did not heed his glance, but with face pale as death she seized a small table and drew it between them and cried: "Throw then, my lord! We know the stakes."

"If you win, Zenda is yours. If I win, you are mine."

"Yes, I and Zenda also," said she. "Throw, my lord!"

"Shall we throw thrice, madame, or once, or how often?"

"Thrice, my lord," she answered, tossing back her hair behind her neck, and holding one hand to her side. "Throw first," she added.

The Count rattled the box; and the throw was seven. Osra took the box from him, looked keenly and defiantly in his eyes, and threw.

"Fortune is with you, madame," said he, biting his lips. "For a five and a four make nine, or I err greatly."

He took the box from her; his hand shook but hers was firm and steady; and again he threw.

"Ah, it is but five," said he impatiently, and a frown settled on his brow.

"It is enough, my lord," said Osra; and pointed to the dice that she had thrown, a three and a one.

The Count's eyes gleamed again; he sprang towards her, and was about to seize the box. But he checked himself suddenly, and bowed saying:

"Throw first this time, I pray you, madame, if it be not disagreeable to you."

"I do not care which way it is," said Osra, and she shook and made her third cast. When she lifted the box, the face of the dice showed seven. A smile broadened on the Count's lips, for he thought surely he could beat seven, he that had beaten eleven and thereby won the Castle of Zenda, which now he staked against the Princess Osra. But his eyes were very keenly and attentively on her, and he held the box poised, shoulder-high, in his right hand.

Then a sudden faintness and sickness seized on the Princess, and the composure that had hitherto upheld her failed; she could not meet his glance, nor could she bear to see the fall of the dice; but she turned away her head before he threw, and stood thus with averted face. But he kept attentive eyes on her, and drew very near to the table so that he stood right over it. And the Princess Osra caught sight of her own face in the mirror, and started to see herself pallid and ghastly, and her features drawn as though she were suffering some great pain. Yet she uttered no sound.

The dice rattled in the box; they rattled on the table; there was a pause while a man might quickly count a dozen; and then Count Nikolas of Festenburg cried out in a voice that trembled and tripped over the words: "Eight, eight, eight!"

But before the last of the words had left his shaking lips, the Princess Osra faced round on him like lightning. She raised her hand so that the loose white sleeve fell back from her rounded arm, and her eyes flashed, and her lips curled as she outstretched her arm at him, and cried:

"Foul play!"

For, as she watched her own pale face in the mirror—the mirror which Count Nikolas had not heeded—she had seen him throw, she had seen him stand for an instant over the dice he had thrown with gloomy and maddened face; and then she had seen a slight swift movement of his left hand, as his fingers deftly darted down and touched one of the dice and turned it. And all this she had seen before he had cried eight.

Therefore now she turned on him, and cried, "Foul play!" and before he could speak, she darted by him towards the door. But he sprang forward, and caught her by the arm above the wrist and gripped her, and his fingers bit into the flesh of her arm, as he gasped, "You lie! Where are you going?" But her voice rang out clear and loud in answer:

"I am going to tell all the world that Zenda is ours again, and I am going to publish in every city in the kingdom that Count Nikolas of Festenburg is a common cheat and rogue, and should be whipped at the cart's tail through the streets of Strelsau. For I saw you in the mirror, my lord, I saw you in the mirror!" And she ended with a wild laugh that echoed through the room.

Still he gripped her arm, and she did not flinch; for an instant he looked full in her eyes; covetousness, and desire, and shame, came all together upon him, and over-mastered him, and he hissed between set teeth:

"You shan't! By God, you shan't!"

"Aye, but I will, my lord," said Osra. "It is a fine tale for the King and for your friends in Strelsau."

An instant longer he held her where she was; and he gasped and licked his lips. Then he suddenly dragged her with him towards a couch; seizing up a coverlet that lay on the couch he flung it around her, and he folded it tight about her, and he drew it close over her face. She could not cry out nor move. He lifted her up and swung her over his shoulder, and, opening the door of the room, dashed down the stairs towards the great hall.

In the great hall were six of the King's Guard, and some of the servants of the Castle, and many of the people who had come with Count Nikolas; they all sprang to their feet when they saw them. He took no heed of them, but rushed at a run through the hall, and out under the portcullis and across the bridge, which had not been raised since he entered. There at the end of the bridge a lackey held his horse; and he leapt on his horse, setting one hand on the saddle, and still holding Osra; and then he cried aloud:

"My men follow me! To Festenburg!"

And all his men ran out, the King's Guard doing nothing to hinder them, and jumping on their horses and setting them at a gallop, hurried after the Count. He, riding furiously, turned towards the town of Zenda, and the whole company swept down the hill, and, reaching the town, clattered and dashed through it at full gallop, neither drawing rein nor turning to right or left; and again they roused the Bishop of Modenstein, and he turned in his bed, wondering what the rush of mounted men meant. But they, galloping still, climbed the opposite hill and came to the Castle of Festenburg with their horses spent and foundered. In they all crowded, close on one another's heels; the bridge was drawn up; and there in the entrance they stood looking at one another, asking mutely what their master had done, and who was the lady whom he carried wrapped in the coverlet. But he ran on till he reached the stairs, and he climbed them, and entering a room in the gate-tower, looking over the moat, he laid the Princess Osra on a couch, and standing over her he smote one hand upon the other, and he swore loudly:

"Now, as God lives, Zenda I will have, and her I will have, and it shall be her husband whom she must, if she will, proclaim a cheat in Strelsau!"

Then he bent down and lifted the coverlet from her face. But she did not stir nor speak, nor open her eyes. For she had fallen into a swoon as they rode, and did not know what had befallen her, nor where she had been brought, nor that she was now in the Castle of Festenburg, and in the power of a desperate man. Thus she lay still and white, while Count Nikolas stood over her and bit his nails in rage. And it was then just on midnight.

On being disturbed for the third time, the Bishop of Modenstein, whose temper was hot and cost him continual prayers and penances from the mastery it strove to win over him, was very impatient; and since he was at once angry and half asleep, it was long before he could or would understand the monstrous news with which his terrified host came trembling and quaking to his bedside in the dead of the night. A servant-girl, stammered the frightened fellow, had run down half dressed and panting from the Castle of Zenda, and declared that whether they chose to believe her or not—and, indeed, she could hardly believe such a thing herself, although she had seen it with her own eyes from her own window—yet Count Nikolas of Festenburg had come to the Castle that evening, had spoken with Princess Osra, and now (they might call her a liar if they chose) had carried off the Princess with him on his horse to Festenburg, alive or dead none knew, and the men-servants were amazed and terrified, and the soldiers were at their wits' end, talking big and threatening to bring ten thousand men from Strelsau and to leave not one stone upon another at Festenburg, and what not. But all the while and for all their big talk nothing was done; and the Princess was at Festenburg, alive or dead or in what strait none knew. And, finally, nobody but one poor servant-girl had had the wit to run down and rouse the town.

The Bishop of Modenstein sat up in his bed and he fairly roared at the innkeeper:

"Are there no men, then, who can fight in the town, fool?"

"None, none, my lord—not against the Count. Count Nikolas is a terrible man. Please God, he has not killed the Princess by now."

"Saddle my horse," said the Bishop, "and be quick with it."

And he leapt out of bed with sparkling eyes. For the Bishop was a young man, but a little turned of thirty, and he was a noble of the old House of Hentzau. Now some of the Hentzaus (of whom history tells us of many) have been good, and some have been bad; and the good fear God, while the bad do not; but neither the good nor the bad fear anything in the world besides. Hence, for good or ill, they do great deeds and risk their lives as another man risks a penury. So the Bishop, leaving his bed, dressed himself in breeches and boots, and set a black hat with a violet feather on his head, and, staying to put on nothing else but his shirt and his cloak over it, in ten minutes was on his horse at the door of the inn. For a moment he looked at a straggling crowd that had gathered there; then with a toss of his head and a curl of his lip he told them what he thought of them, saying openly that he thanked heaven they were not of his diocese, and in an instant he was galloping through the streets of the town towards the Castle of Festenburg, with his sword by his side and a brace of pistols in the holsters of the saddle. Thus he left the gossipers and vapourers behind, and rode alone as he was up the hill, his blood leaping and his heart beating quick; for, as he went, he said to himself:

"It is not often a Churchman has a chance like this."

On the stroke of half-past twelve he came to the bridge of the

Castle moat, and the bridge was up. But the Bishop shouted, and the watchman came out and stood in the gateway across the moat, and, the night being fine and clear, he presented an excellent aim.

"My pistol is straight at your head," cried the Bishop, "let down the bridge. I am Frederick of Hentzau; that is, I am the Bishop of Modenstein, and I charge you, if you are a dutiful son of the Church, to obey me. The pistol is full at your head."

The watchman knew the Bishop, but he also knew the Count his master.

"I dare not let down the bridge without an order from my lord," he faltered.

"Then before you can turn round, you're a dead man," said the Bishop.

"Will you hold me harmless with my lord, if I let it down?"

"Aye, he shall not hurt you. But if you do not immediately let it down, I'll shoot you first and refuse you Christian burial afterwards. Come, down with it."

So the watchman, fearing that, if he refused, the Bishop would spare neither body nor soul, but would destroy the one and damn the other, let down the bridge, and the Bishop, leaping from his horse, ran across with his drawn sword in one hand and a pistol in the other. Walking into the hall, he found a great company of Count Nikolas's men, drinking with one another, but talking uneasily and seeming alarmed. And the Bishop raised the hand that held the sword above his head in the attitude of benediction, saying, "Peace be with you!"

Most of them knew him by his face, and all knew him as soon as a comrade whispered his name, and they sprang to their feet, uncovering their heads and bowing. And he said:

"Where is your master the Count?"

"The Count is upstairs, my lord," they answered. "You cannot see him now."

"Nay, but I will see him," said the Bishop.

"We are ordered to let none pass," said they, and although their manner was full of respect, they spread themselves across the hall, and thus barred the way to the staircase that rose in the corner of the hall. But the Bishop faced them in great anger, crying:

"Do you think I do not know what has been done? Are you all, then, parties in this treachery? Do you all want to swing from the turrets of the Castle when the King comes with a thousand men from Strelsau?"

At this they looked at him and at one another with great uneasiness; for they knew that the King had no mercy when he was roused, and that he loved his sister above everybody in the world. And the Bishop stepped up close to their rank. Then one of them drew his sword half-way from its scabbard. But the Bishop, perceiving this, cried:

"Do you all do violence to a lady, and dare to lay hands on the King's sister? Aye, and here is a fellow that would strike a Bishop of God's Church!" And he caught the fellow a buffet with the flat of his sword, that knocked him down. "Let me pass, you rogues," said the Bishop. "Do you think you can stop a Hentzau?"

"Let us go and tell the Count that my lord the Bishop is here," cried the house-steward, thinking that he had found a way out of the difficulty; for they dared neither to touch the Bishop nor yet to let him through; and the steward turned to run towards the staircase. But the Bishop sprang after him, quick as an arrow, and, dropping the pistol from his left hand, caught him by the shoulder and hurled him back. "I want no announcing," he said. "The Church is free to enter everywhere." And he burst through them at the point of the sword, reckless now what might befall him so that he made his way through. But they did not venture to cut him down; for they knew that nothing but death would stop him, and for their very souls' sake they dared not kill him. So he, kicking one and pushing another and laying about him with the flat of his sword and with his free hand, and reminding them all the while of their duty to the Church and of his sacred character, at last made his way through and stood alone, unhurt, at the foot of the staircase, while they cowered by the walls or looked at him in stupid helplessness and bewilderment. And the Bishop swiftly mounted the stairs.

At this instant in the room in the gate-tower of the Castle overlooking the moat there had fallen a moment of dead silence. Here Count Nikolas had raised the Princess, set her on a couch, and waited till her faintness and fright were gone. Then he had come near to her, and in brief harsh tones told her his mind. For him, indeed, the dice were now cast; in his fury and fear he had dared all. He was calm now, with the calmness of a man at a great turn of fate. That room, he told her, she should never leave alive, save as his promised wife, sworn and held to secrecy and silence by the force of that bond and of her oath. If he killed her he must die, whether by his own hand or the King's mattered little. But he would die for a great cause and in a great venture.

"I shall not be called a cheating gamester, madame," said he, a smile on his pale face. "I choose death sooner than disgrace. Such is my choice. What is yours? It stands between death and silence; and no man but your husband will dare to trust your silence."

"You do not dare to kill me," said she defiantly.

"Madame, I dare do nothing else. They may write 'murderer' on my tomb; they shall not throw 'cheat' in my living face."

"I will not be silent," cried Osra, springing to her feet. "And rather than be your wife I would die a thousand times. For a cheat you are— a cheat—a cheat!" Her voice rose, till he feared that she would be heard, if any one chanced to listen, even from so far off as the hall. Yet he made one more effort, seeking to move her by an appeal to which women are not wont to be insensible.

"A cheat, yes!" said he. "I, Nikolas of Festenburg, am a cheat. I say it, though no other man shall while I live to hear him. But to gain what stake?"

"Why, my brother's Castle of Zenda."

"I swear to you it was not," he cried, coming nearer to her. "I did not fear losing on the cast, but I could not endure not to win. Not my stake, madame, but yours lured me to my foul play. Have you your face, and yet do not know to what it drives men?"

"If I have a fair face, it should inspire fair deeds," said she. "Do not touch me, sir, do not touch me. I loathe breathing the same air with you, or so much as seeing your face. Aye, and I can die. Even the women of our House know how to die."

At her scorn and contempt a great rage came upon him, and he gripped the hilt of his sword, and drew it from the scabbard. But she stood still, facing him with calm eyes. Her lips moved for a moment in prayer, but she did not shrink.

"I pray you," said he in trembling speech, mastering himself for an instant, "I pray you!" But he could say no more.

"I will cry your cheating in all Strelsau," said she.

"Then commend your soul to God. For in one minute you shall die."

Still she stood motionless; and he began to come near to her, his sword now drawn in his hand. Having come within the distance from which he could strike her, he paused and gazed into her eyes. She answered him with a smile. Then there was for an instant the utter stillness in the room; and in that instant the Bishop of Modenstein set his foot on the staircase and came running up. On a sudden Osra heard the step, and a gleam flashed in her eye. The Count heard it also, and his sword was arrested in its stroke. A smile came on his face. He was glad at the coming of some one whom he might kill in fight; for it turned him sick to butcher her unresisting. Yet he dared not let her go, to cry his cheating in the streets of Strelsau. The steps came nearer.

He dropped his sword on the floor and sprang upon her. A shriek rang out, but he pressed his hand on her mouth and seized her in his arms. She had no strength to resist, and he carried her swiftly across the room to a door in the wall. He pulled the door open—it was very heavy and massive—and he flung her down roughly on the stone floor of a little chamber, square and lofty, having but one small window high up, through which the moonlight scarcely pierced. She fell with a moan of pain. Unheeding, he turned on his heel and shut the door. And, as he turned, he heard a man throw himself against the door of the room. It also was strong and twice the man hurled himself with all his force against it. At last it strained and gave way; and the Bishop of Modenstein burst into the room breathless. And he saw no trace of the Princess's presence, but only Count Nikolas standing sword in hand in front of the door in the wall with a sneering smile on his face.

The Bishop of Modenstein never loved to speak afterwards of what followed, saying always that he rather deplored than gloried in it, and that when a man of sacred profession was forced to use the weapons of this world it was a matter of grief to him, not of vaunting. But the King compelled him by urgent requests to describe the whole affair, while the Princess was never weary of telling all that she knew, or of blessing all bishops for the sake of the Bishop of Modenstein. Yet the Bishop blamed himself; perhaps, if the truth were known, not for the necessity that drove him to do what he did, as much as for a secret and ashamed joy which he detected in himself. For certainly, as he burst into the room now, there was no sign of reluctance or unwillingness in his face; he took off his feathered hat, bowed politely to the Count, and resting the point of his sword on the floor, asked:

"My lord, where is the Princess?"

"What do you want here, and who are you?" cried the Count with a blasphemous oath.

"When we were boys together, you knew Frederick of Hentzau. Do you not now know the Bishop of Modenstein?"

"My lord, where is the Princess?"

"Bishop! This is no place for bishops. Get back to your prayers, my lord."

"It wants some time yet before matins," answered the Bishop. "My lord, where is the Princess?"

"What do you want with her?"

"I am here to escort her wherever it may be her pleasure to go."

He spoke confidently, but he was in his heart alarmed and uneasy because he had not found the Princess.

"I do not know where she is," said Nikolas of Festenburg.

"My lord, you lie," said the Bishop of Modenstein.

The Count had wanted nothing but an excuse for attacking the intruder. He had it now, and an angry flush mounted in his cheeks as he walked across to where the Bishop stood.

Shifting his sword, which he had picked up again, to his left hand, he struck the Bishop on the face with his gloved hand. The Bishop smiled and turned the other cheek to Count Nikolas, who struck again with all his force, so that he reeled back, catching hold of the open door to avoid falling, and the blood started dull red under the skin of his face. But he still smiled, and bowed, saying:

"I find nothing about the third blow in Holy Scripture."

At this instant the Princess Osra, who had been half stunned by the violence with which Nikolas had thrown her on the floor, came to her full senses and, hearing the Bishop's voice, she cried out loudly for help. He, hearing her, darted in an instant across the room, and was at the door of the little chamber before the Count could stop him. He pulled the door open and Osra sprang out to him, saying:

"Save me! Save me!"

"You are safe, madame, have no fear," answered the Bishop. And turning to the Count, he continued:

"Let us go outside, my lord, and discuss this matter. Our dispute will disturb and perhaps alarm the Princess."

And a man might have read the purpose in his eyes, though his manner and words were gentle; for he had sworn in his heart that the Count should not escape.

But the Count cared as little for the presence of the Princess as he had for her dignity, her honour, or her life: and now that she was no longer wholly at his mercy, but there was a new chance that she might escape, his rage and the fear of exposure lashed him to fury, and, without more talking, he made at the Bishop, crying:

"You first and then her! I'll be rid of the pair of you!"

The Bishop faced him, standing between Princess Osra and his assault, while she shrank back a little, sheltering herself behind the heavy door. For although she had been ready to die without fear, yet the sight of men fighting frightened her, and she veiled her face with her hands, and waited in dread to hear the sound of their swords clashing. But the Bishop looked very happy, and, setting his hat on his head with a jaunty air, he stood on guard. For ten years or more he had not used his sword, but the secret of its mastery seemed to revive, fresh and clear in his mind, and let his soul say what it would, his body rejoiced to be at the exercise again, so that his blood kindled and his eyes gleamed in the glee of strife. Thus he stepped forward, guarding himself, and thus he met the Count's impetuous onset; he neither flinched nor gave back, but finding himself holding his own, he pressed on and on, not violently attacking and yet never resting, and turning every thrust with a wrist of iron. And while Osra now gazed with wide eyes and close-held breath, and Count Nikolas muttered oaths and grew more furious, the Bishop seemed as gay as when he talked to the King, more gaily, may be, than Bishops should. Again his eye danced as in the days when he had been called the wildest of the Hentzaus. And still he drove Count Nikolas back and back.

Now behind the Count was a window, which he himself had caused to be enlarged and made low and wide, in order that he might look from it over the surrounding country; in time of war it was covered with a close and strong iron grating. But now the grating was off and the window open, and beneath the window was a fall of fifty feet or hard upon it into the moat below. The Count, looking into the Bishop's face, and seeing him smile, suddenly recollected the window, and fancied it was the Bishop's design to drive him on to it so that he could give back no more; and, since he knew by now that the Bishop was his master with the sword, a despairing rage settled upon him; determining to die swiftly, since die he must, he rushed forward, making a desperate lunge at his enemy. But the Bishop parried the lunge, and, always seeming to be about to run the Count through the body, again forced him to retreat till his back was close to the opening of the window. Here Nikolas stood, his eyes glaring like a madman's; then a sudden devilish smile spread over his face.

"Will you yield yourself, my lord?" cried the Bishop, putting a

restraint on the wicked impulse to kill the man, and lowering his point
for an instant.

In that short moment the Count made his last throw; for all at
once, as it seemed, and almost in one motion, he thrust and wounded
the Bishop in the left side of his body, high in the chest near the
shoulder, and, though the wound was slight, the blood flowed freely;
then drawing back his sword, he seized it by the blade half-way up
and flung it like a javelin at the Princess, who stood still by the door,
breathlessly watching the fight. By an ace it missed her head, and it
pinned a tress of her hair to the door and quivered deep-set in the
wood of the door. When the Bishop of Modenstein saw this, hesitation
and mercy passed out of his heart, and though the man had now no
weapon, he thought of sparing him no more than he would have spared
any cruel and savage beast, but he drove his sword into his body, and
the Count, not being able to endure the thrust without flinching, against
his own will gave back before it. Then came from his lips a loud cry of
dismay and despair; for at the same moment that the sword was in
him he, staggering back, fell wounded to death through the open
window. The Bishop looked out after him, and Princess Osra heard
the sound of a great splash in the water of the moat below; for very
horror she sank against the door, seeming to be held up more by the
sword that had pinned her hair than by her own strength. Then came
up through the window, from which the Bishop still looked with a
strange smile, the clatter of a hundred feet, running to the gate of the
Castle. The bridge was let down; the confused sound of many men
talking, of whispers, of shouts, and of cries of horror, mounted up
through the air. For the Count's men in the hall also had heard the
splash, and run out to see what it was, and there they beheld the body
of their master, dead in the moat; their eyes were wide open, and they
could hardly lay their tongues to the words as they pointed to the
body and whispered to one another, very low: "The Bishop has killed
him—the Bishop has killed him." But the Bishop saw them from the
window, and leant out, crying:

"Yes, I have killed him. So perish all such villains!"

When they looked up, and saw in the moonlight the Bishop's face,
they were amazed. But he hastily drew his head in, so that they might
not see him any more. For he knew that his face had been fierce, and
exultant, and joyful. Then, dropping his sword, he ran across to the
Princess; he drew the Count's sword, which was wet with his own

HE DROVE HIS SWORD INTO HIS BODY, AND THE COUNT GAVE BACK BEFORE IT.

blood, out of the door, releasing the Princess's hair; and, seeing that she was very faint, he put his arm about her, and led her to the couch; she sank upon it, trembling and white as her white gown, and murmuring: "Fearful, fearful!" and she clutched his arm, and for a long while she would not let him go; and her eyes were fixed on the Count's sword that lay on the floor by the entrance of the little room.

"Courage, madame," said the Bishop softly. "All danger is past. The villain is dead, and you are with the most devoted of your servants."

"Yes, yes," she said, and pressed his arm and shivered. "Is he really dead?"

"He is dead. God have mercy on him," said the Bishop.

"And you killed him?"

"I killed him. If it were a sin, pray God forgive me!"

Up through the window still came the noise of voices and the stir of men moving; for they were recovering the body of the Count from the moat; yet neither Osra nor the Bishop noticed any longer what was passing; he was intent on her, and she seemed hardly yet herself; but suddenly, before he could interpose, she threw herself off the couch and on to her knees in front of him, and, seizing hold of his hand, she kissed first the episcopal ring that he wore and then his hand. For he was both Bishop and a gallant gentleman, and a kiss she gave him for each; and after she had kissed his hand, she held it in both of hers as though for safety's sake she clung to it. But he raised her hastily, crying to her not to kneel before him, and, throwing away his hat, he knelt before her, kissing her hands many times. She seemed now recovered from her bewilderment and terror; for as she looked down on him kneeling, she was half-way between tears and smiles, and with curving lips but wet shining eyes, she said very softly:

"Ah, my lord, who made a bishop of you?" And her cheeks grew in an instant from dead white into sudden red, and her hand moved over his head as if she would fain have touched him with it. And she bent down ever so little towards him. Yet, perhaps, it was nothing; any lady, who had seen how he bore himself, and knew that it was in her cause, for her honour and life, might well have done the same.

The Bishop of Modenstein made no immediate answer; his head was still bowed over her hand, and after a while he kissed her hand again; and he felt her hand press his. Then, suddenly, as though in alarm, she drew her hand away, and he let it go easily. Then he raised his eyes and met the glance of hers, and he smiled; and Osra also smiled. For an instant they were thus. Then the Bishop rose to his feet, and he stood before her with bent head and eyes that sought the ground in becoming humility.

"It is by God's infinite goodness and divine permission that I hold my sacred office," said he. "I would that I were more worthy of it! But to-day I have taken pleasure in the killing of a man."

"And in the saving of a lady, sir," she added softly, "who will ever count you among her dearest friends and the most gallant of her defenders. Is God angry at such a deed as that?"

"May He forgive us all our sins," said the Bishop gravely; but what other sins he had in his mind he did not say, nor did the Princess ask him.

Then he gave her his arm, and they two walked together down the stairs into the hall; the Bishop, having forgotten both his hat and his sword, was bare-headed and bad no weapon in his hand. The Count's men were all collected in the hall, being crowded round a table that stood by the wall; for on the table lay the body of Count Nikolas of Festenburg and it was covered with a horse-cloth that one of the servants had thrown over it. But when the men saw the Princess and the Bishop, they made way for them and stood aside, bowing low as they passed.

"You bow now," said Osra, "but, before, none of you would lift a finger for me. To my lord the Bishop alone do I owe my life; and he is a Churchman, while you were free to fight for me. For my part, I do not envy your wives such husbands;" and with a most scornful air she passed between their ranks, taking great and ostentatious care not to touch one of them even with the hem of her gown. At this they grew red and shuffled on their feet; and one or two swore under their breath, and thanked God their wives were not such shrews, being indeed very much ashamed of themselves, and very uneasy at thinking what these same wives of theirs would say to them when the thing came to be known. But Osra and the Bishop passed over the bridge, and he set her on his horse. The summer morning had just dawned, clear and fair, so that the sun caught her ruddy hair as she mounted in her white gown. But the Bishop took the bridle of the horse and led it at a foot's pace down the hill and into the town.

Now by this time the news of what had chanced had run all through the town, and the people were out in the streets, gossiping and guessing. And when they saw the Princess Osra safe and sound and smiling,

HE WALKED WITH HIS HEAD DOWN
AND HIS EYES ON THE GROUND.

and the Bishop in his shirt—for he had given his cloak to her—leading the horse, they broke into great cheering. The men cheered the Princess, while the women thrust themselves to the front rank of the crowd, and blessed the Bishop of Modenstein. But he walked with his head down and his eyes on the ground, and would not look up, even when the women cried out in great fear and admiration on seeing that his shirt was stained with his blood and with the blood of Nikolas of Festenburg that had spurted out upon it. But one thing the Princess heard, which sent her cheeks red again; for a buxom girl glanced merrily at her, and made bold to say in a tone that the Princess could not but hear:

"By the Saints, here's waste! If he were not a Churchman, now!" And her laughing eye travelled from the Princess to him, and back to the Princess again.

"Shall we go a little faster?" whispered Osra, bending down to the Bishop. But the girl only thought that she whispered something else, and laughed the more.

At last they passed the town, and with a great crowd still following them, came to the Castle. At the gate of it the Bishop stopped and aided the Princess to alight. Again he knelt and kissed her hand, saying only:

"Madame, farewell!"

"Farewell, my lord," said Osra softly; and she went hastily into the Castle, while the Bishop returned to his inn in the town, and though the people stood round the inn the best part of the day, calling and watching for him, he would not shew himself.

In the evening of that day the King having heard the tidings of the crime of Count Nikolas, came in furious haste with a troop of horse from Strelsau. And when he heard how Osra had played at dice with the Count, and staking herself against the Castle of Zenda had won it back, he was ashamed, and swore an oath that he would play dice no more, which oath he faithfully observed. But in the morning of the next day he went to Festenburg, where he flogged soundly every man who had not run away before his coming; and all the possessions of Count Nikolas he confiscated, and he pulled down the Castle of Festenburg and filled up the moat that had run round its walls.

Then he sent for the Bishop of Modenstein, and thanked him, offering to him all the demesne of Count Nikolas; but the Bishop would not accept it, nor any mark of the King's favour, not even the

Order of the Red Rose. Therefore the King granted the ground on which the Castle stood, and all the lands belonging to it, to Francis of Tarlenheim, brother-in-law to the wife of Prince Henry, who built the *château* which now stands there and belongs to the same family to this day.

But the Bishop of Modenstein, having been entertained by the King with great splendour for two days, would not stay longer, but set out to pursue his journey, clad now in his ecclesiastical garments. And Princess Osra sat by her window, leaning her head on her hand, and watching him till the trees of the forest hid him; and once, when he was on the edge of the forest, he turned his face for an instant, and looked back at her where she sat watching in the window. Thus he went to Strelsau; and when he was come there, he sent immediately for his confessor, and the confessor, having heard him, laid upon him a severe penance, which he performed with great zeal, exactness, and contrition. But whether the penance were for killing Count Nikolas of Festenburg (which in a layman, at least, would have seemed but a venial sin) or for what else, who shall say?

Chapter VI

The Device of Giraldo the Painter

When the twenty-first birthday of the Princess Osra approached, her brother King Rudolf, desiring to make her a present, summoned from his home at Verona, in Italy, a painter of very high fame, by name Giraldo, and commanded him to paint a portrait of the Princess, to be her brother's gift to her. This command Giraldo carried out, the Princess giving him every opportunity of studying her features and grudging no time that was spent by her in front of his easel; and the picture, when finished, being pronounced to be as faithful as beautiful the reputation of Giraldo was greatly enhanced by the painting of it. Thus it followed that in many cases, when foreign Princes had heard the widespread praises of Osra's beauty, they sent orders to Giraldo to execute for them, and despatch with all speed, miniatures or other portraits of the Princess, that they might judge for themselves whether she were in truth as lovely as report said; and they sent Giraldo large sums of money in recompense, adding not seldom some further donation on the express term and condition that Giraldo should observe absolute fidelity in his representation and not permit himself the least flattery. For some desired themselves to court her, and others intended their sons to ask her hand, if the evidence of Giraldo's portraits satisfied their hopes. So Giraldo, although but two or three years above thirty, grew in both fame and wealth, and was very often indebted to the Princess for the favour of a visit to his house, that he might again correct his memory of her face.

Now what several Princes had done before, it chanced that the King of Glottenberg also did; and Giraldo, to all appearance much pleased, accepted the command, and prayed the Princess to visit him; for, he said, this picture was to be larger and more elaborate than the rest, and therefore needed more study of her. So the Princess went many times, and the portrait destined for the King of Glottenberg (who was said to be seeking a suitable alliance for his eldest son) grew before her eyes into the most perfect and beautiful presentment of her which the skill of Giraldo had ever accomplished, surpassing even that first picture which he had painted by King Rudolf's command. The King made no doubt that, so soon as the picture had reached the Court of Glottenberg, an embassy would come from there to demand the hand of his sister for the Crown Prince, a proposal which he would have received with much pleasure and gratification.

"I do not think," said Osra, tossing her head, "that any such embassy will come, sire. For four or five pictures have been already painted by Signor Giraldo in like manner, but no embassies have come. It seems that my poor features do not find approval in the Courts of Europe."

Her tone, it must be confessed, was full of contempt. For the Princess Osra knew that she was beautiful, as indeed all beautiful ladies are, by the benevolence of heaven, permitted to know. How much greater mischief might they work, if such knowledge were denied them!

"That's true enough," cried Rudolf. "And I do not understand the meaning of it. But it will not be so at Glottenberg. For my good brother the King has eyes in his head, and his son sees no less well. I met them on my travels, and I can speak to it. Most certainly an embassy will come from Glottenberg before we are a month older!"

Yet, strange to say, the same thing followed on the despatch of the portrait (which Giraldo sent by a certain trusty messenger, whom he was accustomed to employ) as had happened before; no embassy came, and the King of Glottenberg excused himself from paying a visit to Strelsau, which he and his son had promised on the invitation of King Rudolf. Therefore Rudolf was very vexed, and Osra also, thinking herself scorned, was very sore at heart, although she bore herself more proudly than before. But, being very greatly disturbed in her mind concerning her beauty, she went herself again to Giraldo and charged him to paint her once more.

"This picture," she said, "is for my own eyes, and mine alone. Therefore, signor, paint it faithfully, and spare me not. For if a woman be ugly, it is well she should know it, and it seems that nobody in the kingdom will tell me the truth, although I get hints enough of it from abroad." And she frowned and flushed and was very sadly out of temper, as any beautiful lady would most naturally be in such a case.

Giraldo bowed very low, seeking to hide the sudden red that dyed his cheek, and to conceal the great joy which the command of the Princess gave him. For by reason of having painted the Princess so often, of having studied her face so curiously, and of having spent so much time in her company, listening to her conversation, and enjoying her wit and grace, this hapless young man had become so deeply and desperately her lover, that he no longer cared to use his brush in the service of any other lady or lord, but stayed at Strelsau solely that he might again and again depict the face that he loved; and, save when she sat before him, he seemed now unable to ply his art at all, and had he not received so many commands for pictures of her, he would have sat all day long idle, thinking of her; which, indeed, was what he did in the intervals between his labour on her portraits. But she, not imagining such presumption and folly on his part, thought that he was glad merely because she would pay him well; so she promised him more and more, if he would but paint her faithfully. And he gave her his word that he would paint her in every respect most faithfully.

"I desire to know," said she, "what I am in truth like; for my mirror says one thing, and the King of Glottenberg—"

But here she stopped, remembering that such matters were not fit for Giraldo's ears. Yet he must have understood, for a strange, cunning, exultant smile came on his lips as he turned away and set himself to mix the colours on his palette. Thus he began this last picture and the Princess came every day and stayed long, so that Giraldo might be able to render her likeness in every most minute respect with perfect fidelity.

"For," she thought resentfully, "either I have no eyes, or they have none in Glottenberg."

When she had been visiting Giraldo thus for hard on a month, and the picture was nearly finished, and was at once the most lovely and the most faithful of all that Giraldo had painted, it chanced that letters came to the King from a nobleman of France who was well known to him, and had known the Princess well also, the Marquis de Mérosailles. And the Marquis wrote to the King in the greatest indignation and scorn, upbraiding the King and saying:

"What is this, sire? Do you keep a madman at your Court, and call him a painter? I have been at Glottenberg; and when I spoke there, as it is my humble duty and true delight to speak everywhere, of the incomparable beauty of your Majesty's sister the Princess Osra, the King, his son, and all the company, did nothing but laugh. I fought three duels with gentlemen of the Court on this account, and two of them I, heaven helping me, wounded, and one, by some devil's trick, wounded me. After this, the matter coming to the King's ear, he sent for me, and excused the laughter by showing me a picture done by a rascal called Giraldo at your Court, the picture was named after your Majesty's most matchless sister; but, as I am a true son of the Church, it was like the devil's daughter, and, on my honour and conscience, it squinted most villainously. I pray you, sire, find out the meaning of this thing; and receive most humble duty and homage from your devoted servant, and, since your graciousness so wills it, most obliged and obedient friend, Henri Marquis de Mérosailles. I kiss the hand of the Princess."

When King Rudolf had read this letter, he grew very thoughtful, and, unknown to Giraldo, he sent and caught the messenger whom Giraldo was wont to entrust with the pictures, and who carried the picture of which M. de Mérosailles wrote to Glottenberg; and the King interrogated the messenger most closely, but got nothing from him, save that he himself never beheld the pictures which he carried, but received them most carefully packed from Giraldo, and so delivered them without undoing the coverings, and then by Giraldo's strict orders returned at once, and did not wait until the recipient had inspected the picture. So that the fellow did not know anything about the picture that had gone to Glottenberg, except that it was certainly the same as Giraldo had entrusted to his hands. But the King was not satisfied and, learning that his sister was at that moment at Giraldo's house, being painted afresh by him, he called half-a-dozen of his gentlemen, and set out on horseback for the place where Giraldo lived in the street that runs from the Cathedral towards the western gate of Strelsau. To this day the house stands there.

The Princess sat and Giraldo painted. Behind the Princess was a window, looking on to the street, and behind Giraldo was a second door, which led into an inner room. On Giraldo's easel stood the nearly finished picture; Giraldo's eyes were alight both with love and with triumph, as he turned from the Princess to the picture, and from the picture to the Princess again; and she, seeing something of his admiration, said with a blush:

"Is it indeed faithful, signor?" For it seemed even to herself a marvellously lovely picture.

"No, madame," answered he. "For my imperfect hand cannot be faithful to perfection."

"I pray you, do not flatter me. Have you indeed shewn every fault of my face?"

"If there be a fault in your face, madame, there it is also in my picture," said Giraldo.

The Princess was silent for a moment, then she said:

"It is better, is it not, than the picture you painted for the King of Glottenberg?"

Giraldo painted a stroke or two before he answered carelessly:

"Indeed, madame, it is more faithful than that which the King of Glottenberg has."

"Then less beautiful?" asked Osra with a petulant smile.

"Nay, I do not say that; not less beautiful," he answered.

"Perhaps he would like this one better, and give me his in exchange; for I never saw his after it was finished. I think I will ask the King to write to him."

Giraldo had turned round suddenly as the Princess made this suggestion; she had spoken half in sport, half in continuing chagrin at the blindness shewn by the Court of Glottenberg. Now he stood staring at her with wide-open alarmed eyes; and he dropped his brushes on to the floor.

"What ails you, signor?" she cried. "I did but suggest exchanging the pictures."

He tried to regain his composure, as he stooped to pick up his brushes.

"The King of Glottenberg's picture is the best for him to have," said he sullenly. "This one, madame, I painted for you yourself, and for you alone."

"I pay the price and can do what I will with the picture," returned the Princess haughtily. "If I desire, I will give it to the King of Glottenberg."

Giraldo had now turned very pale, and, forgetful of the picture, stood gazing fixedly at the Princess. For he could no longer hold down in secrecy and silence the passion that possessed him, but it was declared in his eyes and in the trembling of his limbs; so that the Princess rose from her chair and shrank away from him in alarm, regretting that she had dismissed her ladies, in order to be less restrained in talk with the painter; and she tried to cry out, that they might hear her where they were in an adjoining room, but her cry froze on her lips at the sight of Giraldo's passion. And he cried in a hoarse whisper:

"He shall not have the picture, he shall not have it!" As he spoke he moved nearer to the Princess, who still shrank away from him, being now in very great alarm, and thinking that surely he had run mad. Yet she looked at him, and, looking, saw whence his madness came; and she felt pity for him, and held out her clasped hands towards him, saying in a very soft voice, and with eyes that grew sad and tender:

"Ah, signor, signor, am I always to have lovers, and never a friend?"

At this the unfortunate painter was overcome, and dropping his head between his hands he gave a deep half-stifled sob, and then he cried:

"God's curse on me, for having slandered the beauty that I love!" And then he sobbed again.

But the Princess wondered greatly what he meant by his strange cry, and turned her eyes again on him in bewildered questioning; saying, as she pointed to the picture:

"There is no slander here, signor, unless too much praise be slander."

Giraldo made her no answer in words, but, springing towards her, caught her by the wrist, and drew her across the room to the door behind his easel. With feverish haste he unlocked it and passed through. The Princess, although now free from his grip, followed him in a strange fascination. Giraldo drew the door close behind him; and at that moment the Princess gave a cry, half a scream, half laughter. For facing her she saw, each on its easel, three, four, five, six pictures of herself, each beautiful and painted most lovingly; and the last of the six was the picture that had been painted by order of the King of Glottenberg. For she knew it by the attire, although the face had not been finished when she had last seen it. A sudden enlightenment pierced her mind, and she knew that Giraldo had not sent the pictures for which she had sat to him, but kept them himself, and sent others to his patrons. This strange conviction found its sure confirmation in a seventh easel which stood apart from the rest, on the other side of the room; for it supported what was in all respects a copy of the portrait on which Giraldo was now engaged, save that by cunning touches he had imparted to the face an alien and fearful aspect; for here, although the features had their shape and perfect grace, yet it was the face of a devil that looked out of the canvas, a face that a man would not have gazing at him from the wall on to the bed where he sought to sleep.

But when Giraldo saw her eyes fixed on this picture, he cried:

"That is for you—the other is mine. Are they not your features? The King of Glottenberg should not have even your features. But you shall have them, and if a devil looks out through such a fair mask, is it not so with all fair women that lead men to destruction? There is your true picture, Princess Osra!" And he flung himself on a couch with a mad cry of rage, and then a groan of despair.

The Princess Osra looked at him, and at the beautiful pictures, and then at the picture that was like her and yet like a devil. First she pitied the painter, and then marvelled at the wonderful mad skill, which so transformed her without drawing a line that could be called untrue. Thus thinking, she stood for a while, grave and puzzled. But then the humour struck her, as it struck her House always in great things and in small; it seemed to her most ludicrous that the pictures should all be resting here in Giraldo's house, while the Princes who had commanded portraits of her had received nothing but distorted parodies of her face, to the end that they might be disgusted and, abandoning the alliance they had projected, leave her still at Strelsau, to be painted times out of number and most fruitlessly by this mad painter. And these thoughts gaining the mastery over the others, in spite of the sad plight of unhappy Signor Giraldo, her lips curved into a bow, her eyes gleamed in dancing merriment, and a moment later she broke into a glad gleeful laugh, that rose and rippled, and fell to soft delighted murmurings. As she looked again at the picture that was like her and also like a devil, her mirth grew and grew at the ingenuity of the work and the mocking devilry so cunningly made out of her face. Small wonder was it to her now that the embassies had not come.

The Princess Osra thus stood laughing, and presently Signor Giraldo looked up. When he had listened and looked for a few moments, his wild mood caught the infection from her, so that, springing to his feet, he also began to laugh loudly, like a man who cannot restrain his amusement, but is carried away by it beyond all bounds and restraints. Thus Giraldo laughed loudly, long, and fiercely; for there was madness in his laugh. And the Princess heard the madness; even while she still laughed, her eyes opened in wonder; alarm came on her face, her merry laugh quivered, trembled, choked in her throat, and at last died away into dumbness; yet her lips hung apart frozen in the shape of laughter, while no laughter came. But as her laugh thus ended in mute horror, his grew louder yet and wilder, and its peal rang through the room, as he gasped between his spasms of horrid mirth, "You, you, you!" and pointed at the picture which he had touched to devilishness. But she shrank away, and stood crouched against the wall; for she knew now that he was mad, but did not know to what his fury might next lead him. Then he caught up a knife that lay on the sill of the window, and, now smiling as though in grim quiet amusement, strode across to the row of pictures, and reached up to them., knife in hand. But Osra suddenly sprang forward, crying:

"Do not hurt them."

"These?" he asked, turning to her with a sneer. "These? I'll destroy them all, for they are no longer beautiful to me, but that one only is beautiful, because it is true." And he wrenched his arm away from the detaining hand she had laid upon it. Falling back in terror, she watched him cutting and slashing each of the pictures, until the face was utterly destroyed. And she feared that when he had finished with the pictures, he would turn upon her; therefore she flung herself on the couch, hiding her face for fear of some horrible fate; she murmured low to herself, "Not my face, O God, not my face!" and she pressed her face down into the cushions of the couch, while he, muttering and grumbling to himself, cut the pictures into strips and ribbons, and strewed the fragments at his feet on the floor. This done, he turned to the devil's face that he loved, and poured out to it, as though it had been a cruel idol he worshipped, a flood of wild passionate reproachful words, that Osra shivered to hear, and the purport of which she dared tell none, though for all her prayers she could not herself forget one of them.

At last he came to her again, and plucked her roughly and rudely from the couch where she lay, and dragged her behind him back to the door again and through it; and they stood together in front of the last picture, whose paint was still wet from his hand. The painted face smiled down on the trembling pale girl with its smile of careless serene dignity, so that now even to herself it seemed hardly to be her picture. For it was the true presentment of a King's daughter, and she no better than a helpless frightened girl. It seemed to reproach her; and suddenly she drew herself to her height, and turned on Giraldo, saying: "You shall not touch it."

She stept forward, so that she stood between him and the picture, raising her hand, and forbidding him to approach it with his knife.

And now the picture seemed more to be hers, although while it smiled she frowned.

But at this moment there came through the window that opened on the street the clatter of horses' hoofs. At the sound Giraldo arrested the motion that he had already made to fling himself on the Princess; whether to kill her, or only to thrust her away from in front of the picture she did not know. Running to the window, he looked out, and called in seeming glee: "It is the King come to see my pictures!" And he looked proud and happy. Going to the door of the room, he flung it open, and stood there waiting for the King and the gentlemen who attended the King. They were not long in coming, for Rudolf was full of anger, impatience, and curiosity, and ran swiftly up the staircase. His gentlemen pressed into the room behind him, and Giraldo drew back, keeping his face to the King and bowing again and again. But the King and the rest saw the knife in his hand; and ragged strips of painted canvas hung here and there on his clothes, while the Princess, pale and proud, stood guarding the picture on the easel. The King, in spite of his wonder, was not turned from the purpose which had brought him to the painter's house, but with a quick step darted up to Giraldo and thrust the letter of the Marquis de Mérosailles into his hand, bidding him in a sharp peremptory tone to read it and give what explanation he could of the contents. Giraldo fell to reading it, while the King turned to his sister in order to ask her why she seemed agitated, and stood so obstinately in front of her own picture; but at that instant one of the gentlemen, whose name was Ladislas, gave a cry of surprise; for he had looked through the door into the inner room, and seen the havoc and destruction that Giraldo had made, and also the strange and terrible picture which alone had escaped the knife. The King, wondering, followed Ladislas to the threshold of the inner room and passed it, while his gentlemen, full of curiosity, crowded close on his heels after him.

The Princess Osra, thinking herself safe, found her anger and terror pass away as her mirth had passed before. Now she felt in her heart that pity which borders on tenderness, and which she could never refuse to a man who loved her, let the folly of his love and of the extravagances into which it drove him be as great as it would. Turning towards Giraldo, she saw him fretting his puckered brow with his hand, and vainly seeking to compel his disordered brain to understand M. de Mérosailles' letter. So she was very sorry for him, and, knowing the sudden hot temper to which the careless King was subject, she glided swiftly across to the painter, and whispered: "Escape and hide. Hide for a few days. He will be furious now, but he will soon forget. Don't wait now, but escape, signor. Some harm will happen to you here;" and in her eager pleading with him she laid her hand on his arm, and looked up in his face with imploring eyes. But he looked at her with dazed vacant stare, muttering, "I cannot read the letter;" then a wistful smile came on his face, and he thrust the letter towards her, saying: "Madame, will you read it for me?" And at that moment they heard the King swear an angry oath; for he had seen the mad picture of his sister.

"No, no, not now," whispered Osra, beseeching Giraldo. "Not now, signor. Listen, the King is angry! Escape now, and we will read the letter afterwards." She was as earnest as though she had loved him and were praying him to save himself for the sake of her love.

Giraldo looked into her softened eyes; suddenly giving a little cry, as if a great joy had come to him unexpectedly and contrary to all likelihood, he dropped M. de Mérosailles' letter, and sprang to where his brushes lay on the floor; seizing them and his palette, he gave another swift glance at the Princess, and then, turning to the picture, began to paint with marvellous dexterity and deftness and with the sudden confidence of a man inspired to the work. As he worked, his brow grew smoother, the tension of his strained face relaxed, happiness dawned in his eyes, and a smile broke on his lips; and Osra watched him with a tender sorrowful gaze. Still he painted, and he was painting when the King burst in from the other room in a great rage, carrying his sword drawn in his hand; for he had sworn by Our Lady and St. Peter to kill the rogue who had done the Princess such wrong and so slandered her beauty. And his gentlemen came in with him, all very ready to see Giraldo killed, but each eager that the King should leave the task to him. Yet when they entered and saw Giraldo painting as though he were rapt by some ecstasy and had forgotten all that had passed, nay, even their very presence, they paused in unwilling and constrained hesitation. Osra raised her hand to bid them stay still where they were, and not interfere with Giraldo's painting. For now she desired above all things on earth that he should be left to finish his task. For he thought that he had read more than pity and more than tenderness in Osra's eyes; he had seemed to see love there, and thus he had cried out in joy, and thus he was now painting as never had even he, for all his skill, painted before. His unerring hand, moving lightly to and fro, imparted the sweetness of his delusive vision to the canvas so that the eyes of the portrait glowed with wonderful and beautiful love and gentleness. Presently Giraldo began to sing very softly to himself a sweet happy old song, that peasants sang to peasant girls in the fields outside his native Verona on summer evenings. His head was thrown back in triumph and exultation as he sang and worked, tasting the luxury of love, and glorying in the tribute that his genius paid to her whom he loved. Thus came a moment of great joy to the soul of Giraldo the painter; for a man's love and a man's work are, when they seem to prosper, of all things the sweetest, and their union in one his life's consummation.

It was done. He laid down the brush, and drew back a step, looking at what he had done. The Princess came softly and slowly, as though attracted against her will, and she stood by him; for she saw that this picture was now, beyond all compare, the most perfect and beautiful of all that he or any other man had painted of her; and she loved him for thus glorifying her. But, before many moments had gone by, a sudden start and shiver ran through Giraldo's body. The spell of his entranced ecstasy broke; his eyes fell from the masterpiece that he had made, and wandered to those who stood about him—to the gentlemen who did not know whether to wonder or to laugh, to the angry face of the King and the naked sword in his hand, at last to Osra, whose eyes were still on the picture. His exultation vanished, and with it went, as it seemed to them, his madness. Reason dawned for a moment in his eyes, but was quenched in an instant by shame and despair. For he knew that all there had seen that other picture and knew now what he had done and suddenly with a stifled cry he flung himself full length on the floor at Osra's feet.

"Let us wait," said she gently. "He will be himself again soon."

But the King was too angry to listen.

"He has made us fools before half Europe," he cried angrily, "and he shall not live to talk of it. And you—have you seen the picture yonder?"

"Yes, I have seen it," said she. "But he does not now think that picture like me, but this one." And she turned to the gentlemen, and desired them to raise Giraldo and lay him on a couch, and they obeyed. Then she knelt by his head; and, after a while he opened his eyes, seeming sound of sense in everything except that he believed she loved him, so that he began to whisper to her as lovers whisper to their loves, very tenderly and low. And the King, with his gentlemen, stood a little way off. But the Princess said nothing to Giraldo, neither refusing his love, nor yet saying what was false; yet she suffered him to talk to her, and to reach up his hand and gently touch a lock of hair that strayed on her forehead. And he, sighing in utter happiness and contentment, closed his eyes again, and lay back very quietly on the couch.

"Let us go," said she rising. "I will send a physician." And she bade one of the gentlemen lock the inner room, and give her the key, and she and the King and they all then departed, and sent his servants to tend Giraldo; and Osra caused the King's physician also to be summoned. But Giraldo did no more than linger some few days alive; for the most of them he was in a high fever, his brain being wild; and he raved about the Princess, sometimes railing at her, sometimes praising her; yet once or twice he awoke, calm and happy as he had been when she knelt by him, and having for his only delusion the thought that she still knelt there and was breathing words of love into his ear. And in this last merciful error, in respect of which the physicians humoured him, one day a week later, he passed away and was at peace.

Then the Princess came, attended by one gentleman in whom she placed confidence, and she destroyed the evil picture that Giraldo had painted, and having caused a fire to be made, burnt up the pieces of it, and all the ruins of the pictures that Giraldo had destroyed. But that on which he had last worked so happily, and with such a triumph of art, she carried with her to the palace; and presently she caused copies to be made of it, and sent one to each of the Princes by whom Giraldo had been commanded to paint her picture, and with it the money he had received, the whole of which was found untouched in a cabinet in his house. But the picture itself she hung in her own chamber, and would often look at it, feeling great sorrow for the fate of Giraldo the painter.

Yet King Rudolf could not be prevailed upon to pity the young man, saying that for his part he should have to be mad before the love of a woman should drive him mad; and he cursed Giraldo for an insolent knave, declaring that he did well to die of his own accord. And because M. de Mérosailles had gallantly defended his sister's beauty in three duels, he sent him by the hand of a high officer his Order of the Red Rose, which M. de Mérosailles wore with great pride at the Court of Versailles.

But when the copies of the last picture reached the Courts to which they were addressed, together with the money and a brief history of Giraldo's mad doings, the Princes turned their thoughts again to the matter of the alliance, and several embassies set out for Strelsau; so that Princess Osra said, with a smile that was half-sad, half-amused, and very whimsical:

"I am much troubled by reason of the loss of Signor Giraldo my painter."

Chapter VII

The Indifference of the Miller of Hofbau

THERE is a swift little river running by the village of Hofbau, and on the river is a mill, kept in the days of King Rudolf III by a sturdy fellow who lived there all alone; the King knew him, having alighted at his house for a draught of beer as he rode hunting, and it was of him the King spoke when he said to the Queen, "There is, I believe, but one man in the country whom Osra could not move, and he is the Miller of Hofbau." But although he addressed the Queen, it was his sister at whom he aimed his speech. The Princess herself was sitting by, and when she heard the King she said:

"In truth I do not desire to move any man. What but trouble comes of it? Yet who is this miller?"

The King told her where the miller might be found, and he added: "If you convert him to the love of women you shall have the finest bracelet in Strelsau.

"There is nothing, sire, so remote from my thoughts or desires as to convert your miller," said Osra scornfully.

In this, at the moment, she spoke truthfully; but being left alone for some days at the Castle of Zenda, which is but a few miles from Hofbau, she found the time hang very heavy on her hands; indeed she did not know what to do with herself for weariness; and for this reason, and none other at all, one day she ordered her horse and rode off with a single groom into the forest. Coming, as the morning went on, to a wide road, she asked the groom where it led. "To Hofbau, madame," he answered. "It is not more than a mile further on." Osra waited a few moments, then she said: "I will ride on and see the village, for I have been told that it is pretty. Wait here till I return," and she rode on, smiling a little, and with a delicate tint of colour in her cheeks.

Before long she saw the river and the mill on the river; and, coming to the mill, she saw the miller sitting before his door, smoking a long pipe. She called out to him, asking him to sell her a glass of milk.

"You can have it for the asking," said the miller. He was a good-looking fair fellow, and wore a scarlet cap. "There is a pail of it just inside the door behind me." Yet he did not rise, but lay there, lolling luxuriously in the sun. For he did not know Osra, never having been to Strelsau in his life, and to Zenda three or four times only, and that when the Princess was not there. Moreover—though this, as must be allowed, is not to the purpose—he had sworn never again to go so far afield.

Being answered in this manner, and at the same time desiring the milk, the Princess had no choice but to dismount.

This she did, and passed by the miller, pausing a moment to look at him with bright curious eyes, that flashed from under the brim of her wide-rimmed feathered hat; but the miller blinked lazily up at the sun and took no heed of her.

Osra passed on, found the pail, poured out a cup of milk, and drank it. Then, refilling the cup, she carried it to the miller.

"Will you not have some?" said she with a smile.

"I was too lazy to get it," said the miller; and he held out his hand, but did not otherwise change his position.

Osra's brow puckered and her cheek flushed as she bent down, holding the cup of milk so that the miller could reach it. He took and drained it, gave it back to her, and put his pipe in his mouth again. Osra sat down by him and watched him. He puffed and blinked away, never so much as looking at her.

"What have you for dinner?" asked she presently.

"A piece of cold pie," said he. "There's enough for two, if you're hungry."

"Would you not like it better hot?"

"Oh, aye; but I cannot weary myself with heating it."

"I'll heat it," said the Princess; and, rising, she went into the house, and made up the fire, which was almost burnt out; then she heated the pie, and set the room in order, and laid the table, and drew a large jug of beer from the cask. Next she placed an arm-chair ready for the miller, and put the jug by it; then she filled the pipe from the bowl of

He took it and drained it.

tobacco and set a cushion in the chair. All this while she hummed a tune, and from time to time smiled gayly. Lastly, she arranged a chair by the elbow of the miller's chair; then she went out and told him that his dinner was ready; and he stumbled to his feet with a sigh of laziness, and walked before her into the house.

"May I come?" cried she.

"Aye, there is enough for two," said the Miller of Hofbau without looking round.

So she followed him in. He sank into the arm-chair and sat there, for a moment surveying the room which was so neat, and the table so daintily laid, and the pie so steaming hot. And he sighed, saying:

"It was like this before poor mother died." And he fell to on a great portion of pie with which Osra piled his plate.

When he had finished eating—which thing did not happen for some time—she held the jug while he took a long draught; then she brought a coal in the tongs and held it while he lit his pipe from it; then she sat down by him. For several moments he puffed, and then at last he turned his head and looked at Princess Osra; she drooped her long lashes and cast down her eyes; next she lifted her eyes and glanced for an instant at the miller; and, finally, she dropped her eyes again and murmured shyly: "What is it, sir? Why do you look at me?"

"You seem to be a handy wench," observed the miller. "The pie was steaming hot and yet not burnt, the beer was well frothed but not shaken nor thickened, and the pipe draws well. Where does your father dwell?"

"He is dead, sir," said Princess Osra very demurely.

"And your mother?" pursued the miller.

"She also is dead."

"There is small harm in that," said the miller thoughtfully; and Osra turned away her head to hide her smile.

"Are you not very lonely, living here all by yourself?" she asked a moment later.

"Indeed I have to do everything for myself," said the miller sadly.

"And there is nobody to—to care for you?"

"No, nor to look after my comfort," said the miller. "Have you any kindred?"

"I have two brothers, sir; but they are married now, and have no need of me."

The miller laid down his pipe and, setting his elbow on the table, faced Princess Osra.

"H'm!" said he. "And is it likely you will ride this way again?"

"I may chance to do so," said Osra, and now there was a glance of malicious triumph in her eyes; she was thinking already how the bracelet would look on her arm.

"Ah!" said the miller. And after a pause he added: "If you do, come half an hour before dinner, and you can lend a hand in making it ready. Where did you get those fine clothes?"

"My mistress gave them to me," answered Osra. "She has cast them off."

"And that horse you rode?"

"It is my master's; I have it to ride when I do my mistress's errands."

"Will your master and mistress do anything for you if you leave your service?"

"I have been promised a present if—" said Osra, and she paused in apparent confusion.

"Aye," said the miller, nodding sagaciously, as he rose slowly from the armchair. "Will you be this way again in a week or so?" he asked.

"I think it is very likely," answered the Princess Osra.

"Then look in," said the miller. "About half an hour before dinner." He nodded his head again very significantly at Osra, and, turning away, went to his work, as a man goes who would far rather sit still in the sun. But just as he reached the door he turned his head and asked:

"Are you sturdy?"

"I am strong enough, I think," said she.

"A sack of flour is a heavy thing for a man to lift by himself," remarked the miller, and with that he passed through the door and left her alone.

Then she cleared the table, put the pie—or what was left—in the larder, set the room in order, refilled the pipe, stood the jug handy by the cask, and, with a look of great satisfaction on her face, tripped out to where her horse was, mounted, and rode away.

The next week—and the interval had seemed long to her, and no less long to the Miller of Hofbau—she came again, and so the week after; and in the week following that she came twice; and on the second of these two days, after dinner, the miller did not go off to his sacks, but he followed her out of the house, pipe in hand, when she went to mount her horse, and as she was about to mount, he said:

"Indeed you're a handy wench."

"You say much of my hands, but nothing of my face," remarked Princess Osra,

"Of your face?" repeated the miller in some surprise. "What should I say of your face?"

"Well, is it not a comely face?" said Osra, turning towards him that he might be better able to answer her question.

The miller regarded her for some minutes, then a slow smile spread on his lips.

"Oh, aye, it is well enough," said he. Then he laid a floury finger on her arm as he continued: "If you come next week—why, it is but half a mile to church! I'll have the cart ready and bid the priest be there. What's your name?" For he had not hitherto asked Osra's name.

"Rosa Schwartz," said she, and her face was all alight with triumph and amusement.

"Yes, I shall be very comfortable with you," said the miller. "We will be at the church an hour before noon, so that there may be time afterwards for the preparation of dinner."

"That will be on Thursday in next week?" asked Osra.

"Aye, on Thursday," said the miller, and he turned on his heel. But in a minute he turned again, saying: "Give me a kiss, then, since we are to be man and wife," and he came slowly towards her, holding his arms open.

"Nay, the kiss will wait till Thursday. Maybe there will be less flour on your face then." And with a laugh she dived under his outstretched arms and made her escape. The day being warm, the miller did not put himself out by pursuing her, but stood where he was, with a broad comfortable smile on his lips; and so he watched her ride away.

Now, as she rode, the Princess was much occupied in thinking of the Miller of Hofbau. Elated and triumphant as she was at having won from him a promise of marriage, she was yet somewhat vexed that he had not shown a more passionate affection, and this thought clouded her brow for full half an hour. But then her face cleared. "Still waters run deep," she said to herself. "He is not like these Court gallants, who have learnt to make love as soon as they learn to walk, and cannot talk to a woman without bowing and grimacing and sighing at every word. The miller has a deep nature, and surely I have won his heart, or he would not take me for his wife. Poor miller! I pray that he may not grieve very bitterly when I make the truth known to him!" And then, at the thought of the grief of the miller, her face was again clouded;

but it again cleared when she considered of the great triumph that she had won, and how she would enjoy a victory over the King, and would have the finest bracelet in all Strelsau as a gift from him. Thus she arrived at the Castle in the height of merriment and exultation.

It chanced that the King came to Zenda that night, to spend a week hunting the boar in the forest; and when Osra, all blushing and laughing, told him of her success with the Miller of Hofbau he was greatly amused, and swore that no such girl ever lived, and applauded her, renewing his promise of the bracelet; and he declared that he would himself ride with her to Hofbau on the wedding-day, and see how the poor miller bore his disappointment.

"Indeed I do not see how you are going to excuse yourself to him," he laughed.

"A purse of five hundred crowns must do that office for me," said she.

"What, will crowns patch a broken heart?"

"His broken heart must heal itself, as men's broken hearts do, brother!"

"In truth, sister, I have known them cure themselves. Let us hope it may be so with the Miller of Hofbau.

"At the worst I have revenged the wrongs of women on him. It is unendurable that any man should scorn us, be he king or miller."

"It is indeed very proper that he should suffer great pangs," said the King, "in spite of his plaster of crowns. I shall love to see the stolid fellow sighing and moaning like a lovesick courtier."

So they agreed to ride together to the miller's at Hofbau on the day appointed for the wedding, and both of them waited with impatience for it. But, with the bad luck that pursues mortals (even though they be princes) in this poor world, it happened that early in the morning of the Thursday a great officer came riding post-haste from Strelsau to take the King's commands on high matters of State; and, although Rudolf was sorely put out of temper by this untoward interruption, yet he had no alternative but to transact the business before he rode to the miller's at Hofbau. So he sat fretting and fuming, while long papers were read to him, and the Princess walked up and down the length of the drawbridge, fretting also; for before the King could escape from his affairs, the hour of the wedding was already come, and doubtless the Miller of Hofbau was waiting with the priest in the church. Indeed it was one o'clock or more before Osra and the King set out from Zenda, and they had then a ride of an hour and a half; and all this when Osra should have been at the miller's at eleven o'clock.

"Poor man, he will be half mad with waiting and with anxiety for me!" cried Osra. "I must give him another hundred crowns on account of it." And she added, after a pause, "I pray he may not take it too much to heart, Rudolf."

"We must try to prevent him doing himself any mischief in his despair," smiled the King.

"Indeed it is a serious matter," pouted the Princess, who thought the King's smile out of place.

"It was not so when you began it," said her brother; and Osra was silent.

Then about half-past two they came in sight of the mill. Now the King dismounted, while they were still several hundred yards away, and tied his horse to a tree in a clump by the wayside; and when they came near to the mill he made a circuit and approached from the side, and, creeping along to the house, hid himself behind a large water-butt, which stood just under the window; from that point he could hear what passed inside the house, and could see if he stood erect. But Osra rode up to the front of the mill, as she had been accustomed, and, getting down from her horse, walked up to the door. The miller's cart stood in the yard of the mill. but the horse was not in the shafts, and neither the miller nor anybody else was to be seen about; and the door of the house was shut.

"He must be waiting at the church," said she. "But I will look in and make sure. Indeed I feel half afraid to meet him." And her heart was beating rapidly and her face was rather pale as she walked up to the door; for she feared what the miller might do in the passion of his disappointment at learning who she was and that she could not be his wife. "I hope the six hundred crowns will comfort him," she said, as she laid her hand on the latch of the door; and she sighed, her heart being heavy for the miller, and, maybe a little heavy also for the guilt that lay on her conscience for having deceived him.

Now when she lifted the latch and opened the door, the sight that met her eyes was this: The table was strewn with the remains of a brave dinner; two burnt-out pipes lay beside the plates. A smaller table was in front of the fire; on it stood a very large jug, entirely empty, but bearing signs of having been full not so long ago; and on either side of it, each in an armchair, sat the priest of the village and the Miller of

Hofbau; both of them were sleeping very contentedly, and snoring somewhat as they slept. The Princess, smitten by remorse at the spectacle, said softly:

"Poor fellow, he grew weary of waiting, and hungry, and was compelled to take his dinner; and, like the kind man he is, he has entertained the priest, and kept him here, so that no time should be lost when I arrived. Indeed I am afraid the poor man loves me very much. Well, miller, or lord, or prince—they are all the same. Heigh-ho! Why did I deceive him?" And she walked up to the miller's chair, leant over the back of it, and lightly touched his red cap with her fingers. He put up his hand and brushed with it, as though he brushed away a fly, but gave no other sign of awakening.

The King called softly from behind the water-butt under the window:

"Is he there, Osra? Is he there?"

"The poor man has fallen asleep in weariness," she answered. "But the priest is here, ready to marry us. Oh, Rudolf, I am so sorry for what I have done!"

"Girls are always mighty sorry, after it is done," remarked the King. "Wake him up, Osra."

At this moment the Miller of Hofbau sat up in his chair and gave a great sneeze; and by this sound the priest also was awakened. Osra came forward and stood between them. The miller looked at her, and tilted his red cap forward in order that he might scratch his head. Then he looked across to the priest, and said:

"It is she, Father. She has come."

The priest rubbed his hands together, and smiled uncomfortably.

"We waited two hours," said he, glancing at the clock. "See, it is three o'clock now."

"I am sorry you waited so long," said Osra, "but I could not come before. And—and now that I am come, I cannot—" But here she paused in great distress and confusion, not knowing how to break her sad tidings to the Miller of Hofbau.

The miller drew his legs up under his chair, and regarded Osra with a grave air.

"You should have been here at eleven," said he. "I went to the church at eleven, and the priest was there, and my cousin Hans to act as my groom, and my cousin Gertrude to be your maid. There we waited hard on two hours. But you did not come."

ON EITHER SIDE OF IT SAT THE PRIEST OF THE VILLAGE
AND THE MILLER OF HOFBAU.

"I am very sorry," pleaded Princess Osra. The King laughed low to himself behind the water-butt, being much amused at her distress and her humility.

"And now that you are come," pursued the miller, scratching his head again, "I do not know what we are to do." He looked again at the priest, seeking counsel.

At this the Princess Osra, thinking that an opportunity had come, took the purse of six hundred crowns from under her cloak, and laid it on the table.

"What is this?" said the miller, for the first time showing some eagerness.

"They are for you," said Osra as she watched him while he unfastened the purse. Then he poured the crowns out on the table, and counted them one by one, till he had told all the six hundred. Then he raised his hands above his head, let them fall again, sighed slightly, and looked across at the priest.

"I warned you not to be in such a hurry, friend miller," remarked the priest.

"I waited two hours," said the miller plaintively, "and you know that she is a handy wench, and very fond of me."

He began to gather up the crowns and return them to the purse.

"I trust I am a handy wench," said Osra, smiling, yet still very nervous, "and, indeed, I have a great regard for the miller, but—"

"Nay, he does not mean you," interrupted the priest.

"Six hundred," sighed the miller, "and Gertrude has but two hundred! Still she is a handy wench and very sturdy. I doubt if you could lift a sack by yourself, as she can." And he looked doubtfully at Osra's slender figure.

"I do not know why you talk of Gertrude," said the Princess petulantly. "What is Gertrude to me?"

"Why, I take it that she is nothing at all to you," answered the priest, folding his hands on his lap and smiling placidly. "Still, for my part, I bade him wait a little longer."

"I waited two hours," said the miller. "And Gertrude urged me, saying that you would not come, and that she would look after me better than you, being one of the family. And she said it was hard that she should have no husband, while her own cousin married a stranger. And since it was all the same to me, provided I got a handy and sturdy wench—"

"What?" cried the Princess Osra; and the King was so interested that he rose up from behind the water-butt, and, leaning his elbows on the window-sill, looked in and saw all that happened.

"It being," pursued the Miller of Hofbau, "all the same to me, so that I got what I wanted, why, when you did not come—"

"He married his cousin," said the priest.

A sudden roar of laughter came from the window. All three turned round, but the King ducked his head and crouched again behind the water-butt before they saw him.

"Who was that?" cried the priest.

"A lad that came to hold my horse," answered Osra hastily, and then she turned fiercely on the miller.

"And that," she said, "was all you wanted! I thought you loved me."

"Aye, I liked you very well," said the miller. "You are a handy—" A stamp of her foot drowned the rest. "But you should have come in time," he went on.

"And this Gertrude—is she pretty?" demanded Osra.

"Gertrude is well enough," said the miller. "But she has only two hundred crowns." And he put the purse, now full again, on the table with a resigned sigh.

"And you shall have no more," cried Osra, snatching up her purse in great rage. "And you and Gertrude may—"

"What of Gertrude?" came at this moment from the door of the room where the sacks were. The Princess turned round swift as the wind, and she saw in the doorway a short and very broad girl, with a very wide face and straggling hair; the girl's nose was very flat, and her eyes were small; but her great mouth smiled good-humouredly and, as the Princess looked, she let slip to the ground a sack of four that she had been carrying on her sturdy back.

"Aye, Gertrude is well enough," said the miller, looking at her contentedly. "She is very strong and willing."

Then, while Gertrude stood wondering and staring with wide eyes in the doorway, the Princess swept up to the miller, and leant over him, and cried:

"Look at my face, look at my face! What manner of face is it?"

"It is well enough," said the miller. "But Gertrude is—"

There was a crash on the floor, and the six hundred crowns rolled out of the purse, and scattered, spinning and rolling hither and thither all over the floor and into every corner of the room. And Princess

Osra cried: "Have you no eyes?" and then she turned away; for her lip was quivering, and she would not have the miller see it. But she turned from the miller only to face Gertrude his wife; Gertrude's small eyes brightened with sudden intelligence.

"Ah, you're the other girl!" said Gertrude with much amusement. "And was that your dowry? It is large! I am glad you did not come in time. But see, I'll pick it up for you. Nay, don't take on. I dare say you'll find another husband."

She passed by Osra, patting her on the shoulder kindly as she went, and then fell on her knees and began to pick up the crowns, crawling after them all over the floor, and holding up her apron to receive the recovered treasure. And Princess Osra stood looking at her.

"Aye, you'll find another husband," nodded the priest encouragingly.

"Aye, you'll find another husband," assented the miller placidly. "And just as one girl is pretty nearly as good as another—if she is handy and sturdy—so one husband is as good as another, if he can keep a house over you."

Princess Osra said nothing. But Gertrude, having picked up the crowns, came to her with a full apron, saying:

"Hold your lap, and I'll pour them in. They'll get you a good husband."

Princess Osra suddenly bent and kissed Gertrude's cheek, and she said gently:

"I hope you have got a good husband, my dear; but let him do some work for himself. And keep the six hundred crowns as a present from me, for he will value you more with eight hundred than with two."

The eyes of all three were fixed on her in wonder and almost in fear, for her tone and manner were now different. Then she turned to the miller, and she bit her lip and dashed her hand across her eyes, and she said:

"And you, miller, are the only sensible man I have found in all the kingdom. Therefore good luck and a good wife to you." And she gave a little short laugh, and turned and walked out of the cottage, leaving them all spellbound in wonder. But the miller rose from his chair and ran to the door, and when he reached it the King was just lifting Osra on to her horse; the miller knew the King, and stood there with eyes wide and cheeks bulged in wonder; but he could gasp out no more than "The King, the King!" before Rudolf and Osra were far away. And they could, none of them, neither the miller, nor Gertrude, nor the priest, tell what the matter meant, until one day King Rudolf rode again to the mill at Hofbau, and, having sent for the priest, told the three enough of the truth, saying that the affair was the outcome of a jest at Court; and he made each of them a handsome present, and vowed them to secrecy by their fealty and attachment to his person and his honour.

"So she would not have married me, anyhow?" asked the miller.

"I think not, friend," answered Rudolf with a laugh.

"Then we are but quits and all is well. Gertrude, the jug, my lass!"

And so, indeed, it seemed to the King that they were but quits, and so he said to the Princess Osra. But he declared that she had so far prevailed with the miller as to make him desire marriage as an excellent and useful thing in itself, although she had not persuaded him that it was of great moment whom a man married. Therefore he was very anxious to give her the bracelet which he had promised, and more than once prayed her to accept it. But Osra saw the laugh that lurked in the King's eye, and would not consent to have the bracelet, and for a long while she did not love to speak of the Miller of Hofbau. Yet once, when the King on some occasion cried out very impatiently that all men were fools, she said:

"Sire, you forget the Miller of Hofbau." And she blushed, and laughed, and turned her eyes away.

One other thing she did which very greatly puzzled Queen Margaret, and all the ladies of the Court, and all the waiting-women, and all the serving-maids, and, in fine, every person high or low who saw or heard of it, except the King only. For in winter evenings she took her scissors and her needle, and she cut strips of ribbon, each a foot long and a couple of inches broad; on each of them she embroidered a motto or legend; and she affixed the ribbons bearing the legend to each and every one of the mirrors in each of her chambers at Strelsau, at Zenda, and at the other royal residences. And her waiting-women noticed that, whenever she had looked in the mirror and smiled at her own image or shewn other signs of pleasure in it, she would then cast her eyes up to the legend, and seem to read it, and blush a little, and laugh a little, and sigh a little; the reason for which things they could by no means understand.

Chapter VIII

The Love of the Prince of Glottenberg

It was the spring of the year when Ludwig, Prince of Glottenberg, came courting the Princess Osra; for his father had sought the most beautiful lady of a Royal House in Europe, and had found none equal to Osra. Therefore the Prince came to Strelsau with a great retinue, and was lodged in the White Palace, which stood on the outskirts of the city, where the public gardens now are (for the Palace itself was sacked and burnt by the people in the rising of 1848). Here Ludwig stayed many days, coming every day to the King's palace to pay his respects to the King and Queen, and to make his court to the Princess. King Rudolf had received him with the utmost friendship, and was, for reasons of State then of great moment but now of vanished interest, as eager for the match as was the King of Glottenberg himself; and he grew very impatient with his sister when she hesitated to accept Ludwig's hand, alleging that she felt for him no more than a kindly esteem, and, what was as much to the purpose, that he felt no more for her. For although the Prince possessed most courteous and winning manners, and was very accomplished both in learning and in exercises, yet he was a grave and pensive young man, rather stately than jovial, and seemed in the Princess's eyes (accustomed as they were to catch and check ardent glances), to perform his wooing more as a duty of his station than on the impulse of any passion. Finding in herself also no such sweet ashamed emotions as had before now invaded her heart on account of lesser men, she grew grave and troubled. At last she said to the King:

"Brother, is this love? For I had as lief he were away as here, and when he is here he kisses my hand as though it were a statue's hand; and—and I feel as though it were. They say you know what love is. Is this love?"

"There are many forms of love," smiled the King. "This is such love as a Prince and a Princess may most properly feel."

"I do not call it love at all," said Osra with a pout.

When Prince Ludwig came next day to see her and told her with grave courtesy that his pleasure lay in doing her will, she broke out:

"I had rather it lay in watching my face," and then, ashamed, she turned away from him.

He seemed grieved and hurt at her words; it was with a sigh that he said:

"My life shall be spent in giving you joy." She turned round on him with flushed cheek and trembling lips:

"Yes, but I had rather it were spent in getting joy from me."

He cast down his eyes a moment, and then, taking her hand, kissed it. But she drew it away sharply. So that afternoon they parted, he back to his Palace, she to her chamber, where she sat, asking again:

"Is this love?" and crying: "He does not know love," and pausing, now and again, before her mirror, to ask her pictured face why it would not unlock the door of love.

On another day she would be merry, or feign merriment, rallying him on his sombre air and formal compliments, professing that for her part she soon grew weary of such wooing, and loved to be easy and merry; for thus she hoped to sting him, so that he would either disclose more warmth or altogether forsake his pursuit. But he offered many apologies, blaming nature that had made him grave, but assuring her of his deep affection and respect.

"Affection and respect!" murmured Osra with a little toss of her head. "Oh, that I had not been born a Princess!" And yet, though she did not love him, she thought him a very noble gentleman, and trusted to his honour and sincerity in everything. Therefore, when he still persisted, and Rudolf and the Queen urged her, telling her (the King mockingly, the Queen with a touch of sadness) that she must not look to find in the world such love as romantic girls dreamt of, at last she yielded; she told her brother that she would marry Prince Ludwig; yet for a little while she would not have the news proclaimed. So Rudolf went, alone and privately, to the White Palace, and said to Ludwig:

"Cousin, you have won the fairest lady in the world. Behold, her brother says it!"

Prince Ludwig bowed low, and taking the King's hand, pressed it, thanking him for his help and approval, and expressing himself as most grateful for the boon of the Princess's favour.

"Will you not come with me and find her?" cried the King with a merry look.

"I have urgent business now," answered Ludwig. "Beg the Princess to forgive me. This afternoon I will crave the honour of waiting on her with my humble gratitude." King Rudolf looked at him, a smile curling on his lips; and he said, in one of his gusts of impatience:

"By heaven! is there another man in the world who would talk about gratitude, and business, and the afternoon, when Osra of Strelsau sat waiting for him?"

"I mean no discourtesy," protested Ludwig, taking the King's arm, and glancing at him with most friendly eyes. "Indeed, dear friend, I am rejoiced and honoured. But this business of mine will not wait."

So the King, frowning and grumbling and laughing, went back alone and told the Princess that the happy wooer was most grateful, and would come after his business was transacted that afternoon. But Osra, having given her hand, would admit no fault in the man she had chosen, and thanked the King for the message with great dignity. Then the King came to her, and, sitting down by her, stroked her hair, saying softly:

"You have had many lovers, sister Osra, and now comes a husband!"

"Yes, now a husband," she murmured, catching swiftly at his hand; her voice was half caught in a sudden sob.

"So goes the world—our world," said the King, knitting his brows and seeming to fall for a moment into a sad reverie.

"I am frightened," she whispered. "Should I be frightened if I loved him?"

"I have been told so," said the King, smiling again. "But the fear has a way of being mastered then." And he drew her to him, and gave her a hearty brother's kiss, telling her to take courage. "You'll thaw the fellow yet," said the King, "though, I grant you, he is icy enough." For the King himself had been by no means what he called an icy man.

But Osra was not satisfied, and sought to assuage the pain of her heart by adorning herself most carefully for the Prince's coming, hoping to fire him to love. For she thought that if he loved she might, although since he did not she could not. And surely he did not, or all the tales of love were false! Thus she came to receive him very magnificently arrayed. There was a flush on her cheek and an uncertain, expectant, fearful look in her eyes; thus she stood before him, as he fell on his knee and kissed her hand. Then he rose and declared his thanks, and promised his devotion; but as he spoke the flush faded and the light died from her eyes; and when at last he drew near to her and offered to kiss her cheek, her eyes were dead and her face pale and cold as she suffered him to touch it. He was content to touch it but once, and seemed not to know how cold it was; and so, after more talk of his father's pleasure and his pride, he took his leave, promising to come again the next day. She ran to the window when the door was closed on him, and thence watched him mount his horse and ride away slowly, with his head bent and his eyes downcast; yet he was a noble gentleman, stately and handsome, kind and true. The tears came suddenly into her eyes and blurred her sight as she leant watching from behind the hanging curtains of the window. Though she dashed them away angrily, they came again, and ran down her pale cold cheeks, mourning the golden vision that seemed gone without fulfilment.

That evening there came a gentleman from the Prince of Glottenberg, carrying most humble excuses from his master, who (so he said) was prevented from waiting on the Princess the next day by a certain very urgent affair which took him from Strelsau, and would keep him absent from the city all day long; and the gentleman delivered to Osra a letter from the Prince, full of graceful and profound apologies, and pleading an engagement that his honour would not let him break; for nothing short of that, said he, should have kept him from her side. There followed some lover's phrases, scantily worded and frigid in an assumed passion. But Osra, smiling graciously, sent back a message, readily accepting all that the Prince urged in excuse. And she told what had passed to the King, with her head high in the air and a careless haughtiness, so that even the King did not rally her, nor yet venture to comfort her, but urged her to spend the day in riding with the Queen and him; for they were setting out for Zenda, where the King was to hunt in the forest, and she could ride some part of the way with them, and return in the evening. And she, wishing that she had sent first to the Prince to bid him not come, agreed to go with her brother; it was better far to go than to wait at home for a lover who would not come.

Thus the next morning they rode out, the King and Queen with their retinue, the Princess attended by one of her Guard, named Christian Hantz, who was greatly attached to her and most jealous in praise and admiration of her. This fellow had taken it on himself to be very angry with Prince Ludwig's coldness, but dared say nothing of it; yet, impelled by his anger, he had set himself to watch the Prince very closely; and thus he had, as he conceived; discovered something which brought a twinkle into his eye and a triumphant smile to his lips as he rode behind the Princess. Some fifteen miles she accompanied her brother, and then, turning with Christian, took another way back to the city. Alone she rode her mind full of sad thoughts; while Christian, behind, still wore his malicious smile. But presently, although she had not commanded him, he quickened his pace and came up to her side, relying for excuse on the favour which she always shewed him.

"Well, Christian," said she, "have you something to say to me?"

For answer he pointed to a small house standing among the trees, some way from the road, and he said:

"If I were Ludwig and not Christian, yet I would be here where Christian is, and not there where Ludwig is," and he pointed still at the house.

She faced round in anger at his daring to speak to her of the Prince, but he was a bold fellow and would not be silenced now that he had begun to speak; he knew also that she would bear much from him. So he leant over towards her, saying:

"By your bounty, madame, I have money, and he who has money can get knowledge. So I know that the Prince is there. For fifty crowns I gained a servant of his, and he told me."

"I do not know why you should spy on the Prince," said Osra, "and I do not care to know where the Prince is;" and she touched her horse with the spur and cantered forward fast, leaving the little house behind. But Christian persisted, partly in a foolish grudge against any man who should win what was above his reach, partly in an honest anger that she, whom he worshipped, should be treated lightly by another; and he forced her to hear what he had learnt from the gossip of the Prince's groom, telling it to her in hints and half-spoken sentences, yet so plainly that she could not miss the gist of it.

She rode the faster towards Strelsau, at first answering nothing; but at last she turned on him fiercely, saying that he told a lie, and that she knew it was a lie, since she knew where the Prince was, and what business had taken him away; and she commanded Christian to be silent and to speak neither to her nor to any one else of his false suspicions; and she bade him very harshly to fall back and ride behind her again, which he did, sullen yet satisfied. For he knew that his arrow had gone home. On she rode, with her cheeks aflame and her heart beating, until she came to Strelsau; having arrived at the Palace, she ran to her own bedroom and flung herself on the bed.

Here for an hour she lay; then, it being about six o'clock, she sat up, pushing her disordered hair back from her hot aching brow. An agony of humiliation had come upon her, and a fury of resentment against the Prince, whose coldness seemed now to need no more explanation. Yet she could hardly believe what she had been told of him, for though she had not loved him, she had accorded to him her full trust. Rising, she paced in pain about the room. She could not rest; she cried out in longing that her brother were there, to aid her and find out the truth for her. But he was away, and she had none to whom she could turn. So she strove to master her anger and endure her suspense till the next day, but they were too strong for her, and she cried:

"I will go myself, I cannot sleep till I know. But I cannot go alone. Who will go with me?" But she knew of none, for she would not take Christian with her, and she shrank from speaking of the matter to any gentlemen of the Court. Yet she must know. At last she sprang from the chair into which she had sunk despondent, exclaiming:

"He is a gentleman and my friend. He will go with me." And she sent hastily for the Bishop of Modenstein, who was then in Strelsau, bidding him come dressed for riding, with a sword, and on the best horse in his stables. The Bishop came equipped as she bade him, and in very great wonder. But when she told what she wanted, and what Christian had made known to her, he grew grave, saying that they must wait and consult the King, when he returned.

"I will not wait an hour," she cried. "I cannot wait an hour."

"Then I will ride and bring you word. You must not go," he urged.

"Nay, if I go alone I will go," said she. "Yes, I will go and myself fling his falseness in his teeth."

Finding her thus resolved, the Bishop knew that he could not turn her; so, leaving her to prepare herself, he caught Christian Hantz, and charged him to bring their horses to the most private gate of the palace, which opened on a little by-street. Here Christian waited for them with the horses, and they came presently, the Bishop wearing a great slouched hat, and swaggering like a roystering trooper while Osra was closely veiled. The Bishop again imposed secrecy on Christian, and then, they both being mounted, said to Osra: "If you will then, madame, come," and thus they rode secretly out of the city, about seven in the evening, the gate-wardens opening the gate at sight of the Royal Arms on Osra's ring, which she gave to the Bishop in order that he might shew it.

In silence they rode a long way, going at a great speed; Osra's face was set and rigid, for she felt now no shame at herself for going, nor any fear of what she might find, but the injury to her pride swallowed every other feeling; and at last she said, in short sharp words, to the Bishop of Modenstein, having suddenly thrown the veil back from her face:

"He shall not live if it prove true."

The Bishop shook his head. His profession was peace; yet his blood also was hot against the man who had put a slight on Princess Osra.

"The King must know of it," he said.

"The King! The King is not here tonight," said Osra; and she pricked her horse and set him at a gallop. The moon, breaking suddenly in brightness from behind a cloud, shewed the Bishop her face. Then she put out her hand and caught him by the arm, whispering: "Are you my friend?"

"Yes, madame," said he. She knew well that he was her friend.

"Kill him for me, then; kill him for me."

"I cannot kill him," said the Bishop. "I pray God it may prove untrue."

"You are not my friend, if you will not kill him," said Osra; and she turned her face away and rode yet more quickly.

At last they came in sight of the little house standing back from the road; and there was a light in one of the upper windows. The Bishop heard a short gasp break from Osra's lips as she pointed with her whip to the window. Now his own breath came quick and fast; he prayed to God that he might remember his sacred character and his vows and not be led into great and deadly sin, at the bidding of that proud and bitter face; and he clenched his left hand and struck his brow with it.

Thus then they came to the gate of the avenue of trees that led to the house. Here, having dismounted and tied their horses to the gate-post, they stood for an instant, and Osra again veiled her face.

"Let me go alone, madame," he implored.

"Give me your sword, and I will go alone," she answered.

"Here, then, is the path," said the Bishop, and he led the way by the moonlight that broke fitfully here and there through the trees.

"He swore that all his life should be mine," she whispered. "Yet I knew that he did not love me."

The Bishop made her no answer; she looked for none and did not know that she spoke the bitterness of her heart in words which he could hear. He bowed his head and prayed again for her and for himself; for he had found his hand gripping the hilt of his sword. Thus, side by side now, they came to the door of the house, and saw a gentleman standing in front of the door, still but watchful. Osra knew that he was the Prince's Chamberlain.

When the Chamberlain saw them, he started violently and clapped a hand to his sword; but Osra flung her veil on to the ground, and the Bishop gripped his arm as with a vice. The Chamberlain looked at Osra and at the Bishop, and half drew his sword.

"This matter is too great for you, sir," said the Bishop. "It is a quarrel of Princes. Stand aside," and before the Chamberlain could make up his mind what to do Osra had passed by him and the Bishop had followed her.

Finding themselves in a narrow passage, they made out by the dim light of a lamp a flight of stairs that rose from the furthest end of it. The Bishop tried to pass the Princess, but she motioned him back, and walked swiftly to the stairs. In silence they mounted, till they had reached the top of the first stage; and facing them, eight or ten steps further up, was a door. By the door stood a groom "this was the man who had treacherously told Christian of his master's doings; but when he saw suddenly what had come of his disloyal chattering, the fellow turned white as a ghost and came tottering in stealthy silence down the stairs, his finger on his lips.

Neither of them spoke to him, nor he to them. They gave no thought to him, his only thought was to escape as soon as he might; so he passed them, and, going on passed also the Chamberlain, who stood dazed at the house-door, and so disappeared, intent on saving the life he had justly forfeited. Thus the rogue vanished, and what became of him none knew or cared. He showed his face no more at Glottenberg or Strelsau.

"Hark, there are voices!" whispered Osra to the Bishop, raising her hand above her head, as they two stood listening.

The voices came from the door that faced them, the voice of a man and the voice of a woman; Osra's glance at her companion told him that she knew as well as he whose the man's voice was.

"It is true, then," she breathed from between her teeth. "My God, it is true!"

The woman's voice spoke now, but the words were not audible. Then came the Prince's:

"For ever, in life or death, apart or together, for ever."

The woman's answer came no more in words, but in deep low passionate sobs which struck their ears like the distant cry of some brute creature in pain that it cannot understand. Yet Osra's face was stern and cold, and her lips curled scornfully when she saw the Bishop's look of pity.

"Come, let us end it," said she, and with a firm step she began to mount the stairs that lay between them and the door.

Yet once again they paused outside the door, for it seemed as though the Princess could not choose but listen to the passionate words of love that pierced her ears like knives; yet they were all sad, speaking of renunciation, not of happiness.

But at last she heard her own name; then with a sudden start she caught the Bishop's hand, for she could not listen longer. She staggered and reeled as she whispered to him:

"The door, the door, open the door!"

The Bishop, his right hand being across his body and resting on the hilt of his sword, laid his left upon the handle of the door, and turned it. Then he flung the door open wide; at that instant Osra sprang past him, her eyes gleaming like flames from her dead white face. And she stood rigid on the threshold of the room, with the Bishop by her side.

In the middle of the room stood the Prince of Glottenberg; strained in a close embrace, clinging to him, supported by his arms, with head buried in his breast, was a girl of slight and slender figure, graceful though not tall; her body was still shaken by continual struggling sobs. The Prince held her there as though against the world, but raised his head and looked at the intruders with a grave sad air. There was no shame on his face, and hardly surprise. Presently he took one arm from about the lady, and, raising it, motioned to them to be still. Osra took one step forward towards where the pair stood; the Bishop caught her sleeve, but she shook him off. The lady looked up into the Prince's face; with a sudden startled cry she clutched him closer, and turned a terrified face over her shoulder. Then she moaned in great fear, and, reeling, fell against the Prince; she would have sunk to the ground if he had not upheld her, and her eyes closed and her lip dropped, as she swooned away. But the Princess smiled, and, drawing herself to her full height, stood watching while Ludwig bore the lady to a couch and laid her there. Then, when he came back and faced her, she asked coldly and slowly:

"Who is this woman, sir? Or is she one of those who have no names?"

The Prince sprang forward, a sudden anger in his eyes; he raised his hand as if he would have pressed it across her scornful mouth and kept back her bitter words. But she did not flinch; pointing at him with her finger, she cried to the Bishop in a ringing voice:

"Kill him, my lord, kill him."

And the sword of the Bishop of Modenstein was half way out of the scabbard.

"I would to God, my lord," said the Prince in low sad tones, "that God would suffer you to kill me and me to take death at your hands. But neither for you nor for me is the blow lawful. Let me speak to the Princess."

The Bishop still grasped his sword; for Osra's face and hand still commanded him. But at the instant of his hesitation, while the temptation was hot on him, there came from the couch where the lady lay a low moan of great pain. She flung her arms out and turned, groaning again, on her back and her head lay hanging over the side of the couch. The Bishop's eyes met Ludwig's, and with a "God forgive me!" he let the sword slip back, and, springing across the room, fell on his knees beside the couch. He broke the gold chain round his neck and grasped the crucifix which it carried in one hand, while with the other he raised the lady's head, praying her to open her eyes, before whose closed lids he held the sacred image; and he, who had come so near to great sin, now prayed softly but fervently for her life and God's pity on her; for the frailty her slight form showed could not withstand the shock of this trial.

"Who is she?" asked the Princess.

But Ludwig's eyes had wandered back to the couch, and he answered only: "My God, it will kill her."

"I care not," said Osra. But then came another low moan. "I care not," said the Princess again. "Ah, she is in great suffering!" And her eyes followed the Prince's.

There was silence, save for the lady's low moans and the whispered prayers of the Bishop of Modenstein. But the lady opened her eyes, and in an instant, answering the summons, the Prince was by her side, kneeling and holding her hand very tenderly; and he met a glance from the Bishop across her prostrate body. The Prince bowed his head and one sob burst from him.

"Leave me alone with her for a little, sir," said the Bishop, and the Prince, obeying, rose and withdrew into the bay of the window, while Osra stood alone near the door by which she had entered.

A few minutes passed, then Osra saw the Prince return to where the lady was and kneel again beside her; and she saw that the Bishop was preparing to perform his most sacred and sublime office; the lady's eyes dwelt on him now in peace and restfulness, and she held Prince Ludwig's hand in her small hand. But Osra would not kneel; she stood upright, still and cold, as though she neither saw nor heard anything of what passed; she would not pity nor forgive the woman, even if, as they seemed to think, she lay dying. But she spoke once, asking in a harsh voice:

"Is there no physician in the house or near?"

"None, madame," said the Prince.

The Bishop began the office, and Osra stood, dimly hearing the words of comfort, peace, and hope, dimly seeing the smile on the lady's face; for gradually her eyes clouded with tears. Now her ears seemed to hear nothing save the sad and piteous sobs that had shaken the girl as she hung about Ludwig's neck. But she strove to drive away her softer thoughts, fanning her fury when it burnt low, and telling herself again of the insult that she had suffered. Thus she rested till the Bishop had performed the office. But when he had finished it, he rose from his knees and came to where Osra was.

"It was your duty," she said, "but it is none of mine."

"She will not live an hour," said he.

"For she had an affection of the heart, and this shock has killed her. Indeed I think she was half dead for grief before we came."

"Who is she?" broke again from Osra's lip's.

"Come and hear," said he, and she followed him obediently, yet unwillingly, to the couch, and looked down at the lady.

The lady looked at her with wondering eyes, and then she smiled faintly, pressing the Prince's hand, and whispering:

"Yet she is so beautiful." And she seemed now wonderfully happy, so that they three all watched her and were envious, although they were to live and she to die.

"Now God pardon her sin!" said the Princess Osra suddenly, and she fell on her knees beside the couch, crying: "Surely God has pardoned her!"

"Sin she has none, save what clings even to the purest in this world," said the Bishop. "For what she has said to me I know to be true."

Osra answered nothing, but gazed in questioning at the Prince, and he, still holding the lady's hand, began to speak in a gentle voice:

"Do not ask her name, madame. But from the first hour that we knew the meaning of love we have loved one another. And had the issue rested in my hands, I would have thrown to the winds all that kept me from her. I remember when first I met her—ah, my sweet, do you remember? From that day to this in soul she has been mine, and I hers in all my life. But more could not be. Madame, you have asked what love is. Here is love. Yet fate is stronger. Thus I came to Strelsau to woo, and she, left alone, resolved to give herself to God."

"How comes she here, then?" whispered Osra, and she laid one hand timidly on the couch, near to the lady yet not so as to touch even her garments.

"She came here—" he began; but suddenly, to their amazement, the lady, who had seemed dead, with an effort raised herself on her elbow, and spoke in a quick eager whisper, as if she feared time and strength would fail.

"He is a great Prince," she said, "he must be a great King; God means him for greatness, God forbid that I should be his ruin. Ah, what a sweet dream he painted! But praise be to the Blessed Saints who kept me strong. Yet at the last I was weak. I could not live without another sight of his face; and so—I came. Next week I am—I was to take the veil; and I came here to see him once again. God pardon me for it. But I could not help it. Ah, madame, I know you, and I see now your beauty. Have you known love?"

"No," said Osra; and she moved her hand near to the lady's hand.

"When he found me here, he prayed me again to do what he asked; and I was half killed in denying it. But I prevailed, and we were even then parting when you came. Why, why did I come?" For a moment her voice died away in a low soft moan. But she made one more effort; clasping Osra's hand in her delicate fingers, she whispered: "I am going. Be his wife."

"No, no, no," whispered Osra, her face now close to the lady's. "You must live; you must live and be happy."

And then she kissed the lady's lips. The lady put out her arms and clasped them round Osra's neck, and again she whispered softly in Osra's ear. Neither Ludwig nor the Bishop heard what she said, but they heard only that Osra sobbed. Presently the lady's arms relaxed a little in their hold, and Osra, having kissed her again, rose and signed to Ludwig to come nearer; while she, turning, gave her hand to the Bishop, and he led her from the room, and, finding another room near, took her in there, where she sat, silent and pale.

Thus half an hour passed; then the Bishop stole out softly, and presently returned, saying:

"God has spared her the long painful path, and has taken her straight to His rest."

Osra heard him, half in a trance and as if she did not hear; she did not know where he went nor what he did, nor anything that passed, until, as it seemed after a long while, she looked up and saw Prince Ludwig standing before her. He was composed and calm; but it seemed as if half the life had gone out of his face. Osra rose slowly to her feet, supporting herself on an arm of the chair on which she had sat; and, when she had seen his face, she suddenly threw herself on the floor at his feet, crying:

"Forgive me, forgive me!"

"The guilt is mine," said he, "I did not trust you and did by stealth what your nobility would have allowed me to do openly. The guilt is mine." And he offered to raise her. But she rose, unaided, asking with choking voice:

"Is she dead?"

"She is dead," said the Prince, and Osra, hearing it, covered her face with her hands and blindly groped her way back to the chair, where she sat, panting and exhausted.

"To her I have said farewell, and now, madame, to you. Yet do not think that I am a man without eyes for your beauty, or a heart to know your worth. I seemed to you a fool and a churl. I grieved most bitterly, and I wronged you bitterly. My excuse for all is now known. For though you are more beautiful than she, yet true love is no wanderer; it gives a beauty that it does not find, and forges a chain no charms can break. Madame, farewell."

She looked at him and saw the sad joy in his eyes, an exultation

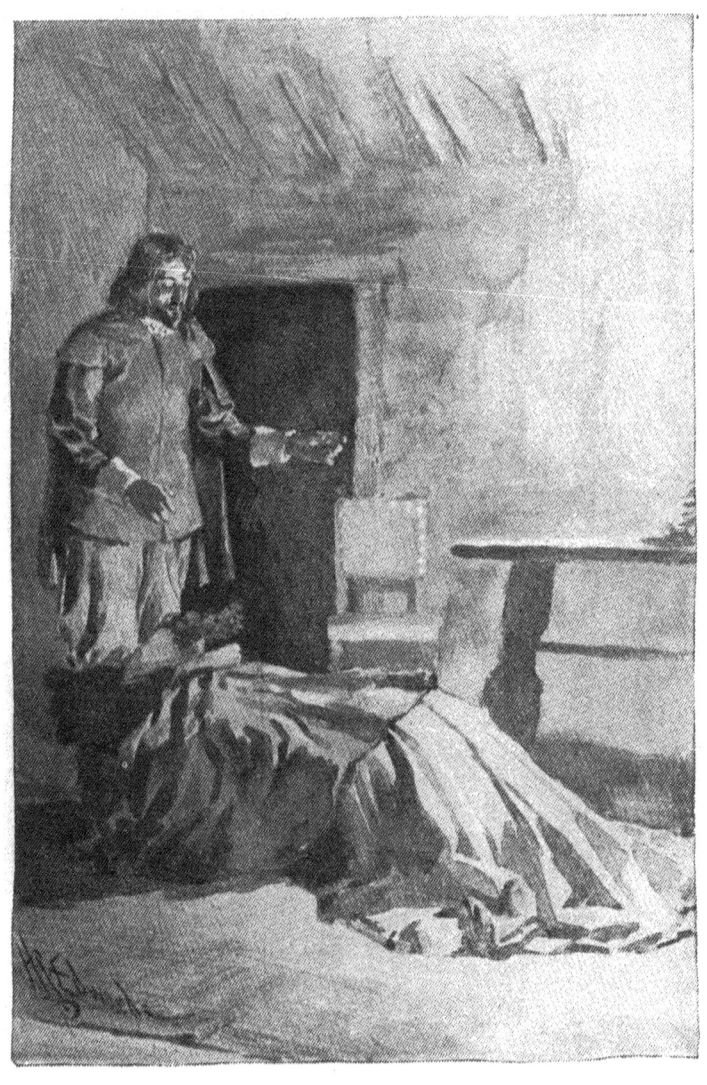

"Forgive me, forgive me!"

over what had been, that what was could not destroy; and she knew that the vision was still with him though his love was dead. Suddenly he seemed to her a man she also might love and for whom she also, if need be, might gladly die; yet not because she loved him, for she was asking still in wonder: "What is this love?"

"Madame, farewell," said he again, and, kneeling before her, he kissed her hand.

"I carry the body of my love," he went on, "back with me to my home, there to mourn for her; and I shall come no more to Strelsau."

Osra bent her eyes on his face as he knelt, and presently she said to him in a whisper that was low for awe, not shame:

"You heard what she bade me do?"

"Yes, madame. I know her wish."

"And you would do it?" she asked.

"Madame, my struggle was fought before she died. But now you know that my love was not yours."

"That also I knew before, sir," and a slight bitter smile came on her face. But she grew grave again and sat there, seeming to be pondering, while Prince Ludwig waited. Then she suddenly leant forward and said:

"If I loved I would wait for you to love. Now what is this love that I cannot feel?"

And then she sat again silent, but at last raised her eyes again to his, saying in a voice that even in the stillness of the room he hardly heard:

"Now I nearly love you, for I have seen your love and know that you can love; and I think that love must breed love, so that she who loves must in God's time be beloved. Yet I—" She paused here, and for a moment hid her face with her hand. "Yet I cannot," she went on. "Is it our Lord Christ who bids us take the lower place? I cannot take it. He does not so reign in my heart. For to my proud heart—ah, my heart so proud!—she would be ever between us. I could not bear it. Yet I believe now that with you I might one day find happiness."

The Prince, though in that hour he could not think of love, was yet very much moved by her new tenderness and felt that what had passed rather drew them together than made any separation between them. And it seemed to him that the dead lady's blessing was on his suit; so he said:

"Madame, I would most faithfully serve you and you would be nearest and dearest to me of all living women."

She waited awhile, then she sighed heavily, looking in his face with
an air of wistful longing; and she knit her brows as though she were
puzzled. But at last, shaking her head, she said:

"It is not enough."

With this she rose and took him by the hand, and they two went
back together to where the Bishop of Modenstein still prayed beside
the body of the lady.

Osra stood on one side of the body and stretched her hand out to
the Prince who stood on the other side.

"See," said she, "she must be between us." And having kissed the
dead face once, she left the Prince there by the side of his love and
herself went out; and, turning her head, she saw that the Prince knelt
again by the corpse of his love.

"He does not think of me," she said to the Bishop.

"His thoughts are still with her, madame," he answered.

It was late night now, and they rode swiftly and silently along the
road to Strelsau. On all the way they spoke to one another only a few
words, both being sunk deep in thought. But once Osra spoke, as they
were already near to Strelsau. For she turned suddenly to the Bishop,
saying:

"My lord, what is it? Do you know it?"

"Yes, madame, I have known it," answered the Bishop.

"Yet you are a Churchman!"

"True, madame," said he, and he smiled sadly.

She seemed to consider, fixing her eyes on his; but he turned his
aside.

"Could you not make me understand?" she asked.

"Your lover, when he comes, will do that, madame," said he, and
still he kept his eyes averted. Osra wondered why he kept his eyes
turned away; yet presently a faint smile curved her lips, and she said:

"It may be you might feel it, if you were not a Churchman. But I do
not. Many men have said they loved me, and I have felt something in
my heart; but not this."

"It will come," said the Bishop.

"Does it come then to every one?"

"To most," he answered.

"Heigho, will it ever come to me?" she sighed.

With this they were at home. And Osra was for a long time very,
sorrowful for the fate of the lady whom the Prince of Glottenberg

had loved; yet, since she saw Ludwig no more, and the joy of youth conquers sadness, she ceased to mourn; but as she walked alone she would wonder more and more what it might be, this great love that she did not feel.

"For none will tell me, not even the Bishop of Modenstein," said she.

Chapter IX

The Victory of the Grand Duke of Mittenheim

King Rudolf, being in the worst of humours, had declared in the presence of all the Court that women were born to plague men and for no other purpose whatsoever under heaven. Hearing this discourteous speech, the Princess Osra rose and said that for her part she would go walking alone by the river outside the city gates, where at least she would be assailed by no more reproaches. For since she was irrevocably determined to live and die unmarried, of what use or benefit was it to trouble her with embassies, courting, or proposals from either the Grand Duke of Mittenheim or anybody else? She was utterly weary of this matter of love, and her mood would be unchanged though this new suitor were as exalted as the King of France, as rich as Croesus himself, and as handsome as the god Apollo. She did not desire a husband, and there was an end of it. Thus she went out, while the Queen sighed, and the King fumed, and the courtiers and ladies said to one another that these dissensions made life very uncomfortable at Strelsau, the ladies further adding that he would be a bold man who married Osra, although doubtless she was not ill-looking.

To the banks of the river outside the walls then Osra went; and as she went she seemed to be thinking of nothing at all in the world, least of all of whom she might chance to meet there on the banks of the river, where in those busy hours of the day few came. Yet there was a strange new light in her eyes, and there seemed a new understanding in her mind; and when a young peasant wife came by, her baby in her arms, Osra stopped her, and kissed the child and gave money, and then ran on in unexplained confusion, laughing and blushing

A young man sprang up, and, with a low bow,
drew aside to let her pass.

as though she had done something which she did not wish to be seen. Then without reason her eyes filled with tears, but she dashed them away and burst suddenly into singing. And she was still singing when, from the long grass by the river's edge, a young man sprang up, and, with a very low bow, drew aside to let her pass. He had a book in his hand, for he was a student at the University, and came there to pursue his learning in peace; his plain brown clothes spoke of no wealth or station, though certainly they set off a stalwart straight shape and seemed to match well with his bright brown hair and hazel eyes. Very low this young man bowed and Osra bent her head. The pace of her walk slowed, grew quicker, slowed again; she was past him, and with a great sigh he lay down again. She turned, he sprang up; she spoke coldly, yet kindly.

"Sir," said she, "I cannot but notice that you lie every day here by the river with your book, and that you sigh. Tell me your trouble, and if I can I will relieve it."

"I am reading, madame," he answered, "of Helen of Troy, and I am sighing because she is dead."

"It is an old grief by now," said Osra, smiling. "Will none serve you but Helen of Troy?"

"If I were a Prince," said he, "I need not mourn."

"No, sir?"

"No, madame," he said, with another bow.

"Farewell, sir."

"Madame, farewell."

So she went on her way, and saw him no more till the next day, nor after that till the next day following; and then came an interval when she saw him not, and the interval was no less than twenty-four hours; yet still he read of Helen of Troy, and still sighed because she was dead, and he no Prince. At last he tempted the longed-for question from Osra's shy smiling lips.

"Why would you not mourn, sir, if you were a Prince?" said she. "For Princes and Princesses have their share of sighs." And with a very plaintive sigh Osra looked at the rapid running river, as she waited for his answer.

"Because then I would go to Strelsau and so forget her."

"But you are at Strelsau now!" she cried with wondering surprise.

"Ah, but I am no Prince, madame," said he.

"Can Princes alone—forget in Strelsau?"

"How should a poor student dare to forget in Strelsau?" As he spoke he made bold to step near her and stood close, looking down into her face. Without a word she turned and left him, going through the meadow with a step that seemed to dance and yet led her to her own chamber, where she could weep in quiet.

"I know it now, I know it now," she whispered softly that night to the tree which rose by her window. "Heigho, what am I to do? I cannot live, no, and now I cannot die. Ah me, what am I to do? I wish I were a peasant girl; but then perhaps he would not—ah, yes, but he would!" And her low long laugh rippled in triumph through the night, blending sweetly with the rustling of the leaves under a summer breeze; and she stretched her white arms to heaven, imploring the kind God with prayers that she dared not speak even to His pitiful ear.

"Love knows no Princesses, my Princess." It was that she heard as she fled from him next day. She should have rebuked him. But for that she must have stayed; and to stay she had not dared. But she must rebuke him. She would see him again in order to rebuke him. Yet all this while she must be pestered with the court of the Grand Duke of Mittenheim! And when she would not name a day on which the embassy should come, the King flew into a passion, and declared that he himself would set a date for it. Was his sister mad, he asked, that she would do nothing but walk every day by the river's bank? "Surely I must be mad," thought Osra; for no sane being could be at once so joyful and so piteously unhappy.

Did he know what it was he asked? He seemed to know nothing of it. He did not speak any more now of Princesses, only of his Princess, nor of Queens, save of his heart's queen; and when his eyes asked love, they asked as though none would refuse and there could be no cause for refusal. He would have wooed his neighbour's daughter thus, and thus he wooed the sister of King Rudolf.

"Will you love me?" was his question, not, "Though you love, yet dare you own your love?" He seemed to shut the whole world from her, leaving nothing but her and him; and in a world that held none but her and him, she could love, unblamed, untroubled, and with no trembling.

"You forget who I am," she faltered once.

"You are the beauty of the world," he answered smiling, and he kissed her hand—a matter about which she could make no great ado, for it was not the first time that he had kissed it.

"You are the beauty of the world,"
he answered smiling.

But the embassy from the Grand Duke was to come in a week and to be received with great pomp. The ambassador was already on the way, carrying proposals and gifts. Therefore Osra went pale and sad down to the river bank that day, having declared again to the King that she would live and die unmarried. But the King had laughed cruelly. Surely she needed kindness and consolation that sad day; yet Fate had kept for her a crowning sorrow; for she found him also almost sad; at least she could not tell whether he was sad or not. For he smiled and yet seemed ill at ease, like a man who ventures a fall with fortune, hoping and fearing. And he said to her:

"Madame, in a week I return to my own country."

She looked at him in silence with lips just parted. For her life she could not speak; but the sun grew dark and the river changed its merry tune to mournful dirges.

"So the dream ends," said he. "So comes the awakening. But if life were all a dream?" His eyes sought hers.

"Yes," she whispered, "if life were all a dream, sir?"

"Then I should dream of two dreamers whose dream was one, and in that dream I should see them ride together at break of day from Strelsau."

"Whither?" she murmured.

"To Paradise," said he. "But the dream ends. If it did not end—" He paused.

"If it did not end?" a breathless longing whisper echoed.

"If it did not end now, it should not end even with death," said he.

"You see them in your dream? You see them riding?"

"Aye, swiftly, side by side, they two alone, through the morning. None is near; none knows."

He seemed to be searching her face for something that yet he scarcely hoped to find.

"Their dream," said he, "brings them at last to a small cottage; it is where they live."

"They live?"

"And work," he added. "For she keeps his home while he works."

"What does she do?" asked Osra, with smiling wondering eyes.

"She gets his supper for him when he comes home weary in the evening, and makes a bright fire, and—"

"Ah, and she runs to meet him at the door! Oh, farther than the door!"

"But she has worked hard and is weary."

"No, she is not weary," cried Osra. "It is for him she works!"

"The wise say this is silly talk," said he.

"The wise are fools then," cried Osra.

"So the dream would please you, madame?" he asked.

She had come not to know how she left him; somehow, while he still spoke, she would suddenly escape by flight. He did not pursue, but let her go. So now she returned to the city, her eyes filled with that golden dream; she entered her home as though it had been some strange Palace decked with unknown magnificence, and she an alien to it. For her true home seemed now rather in the cottage of the dream, and she moved unfamiliarly through the pomp that had been hers from birth. Her soul was gone from it, while her body rested there; and life stopped for her till she saw him again by the banks of the river.

"In five days now I go," said he, and he smiled at her. She hid her face in her hands. Still he smiled; but suddenly he sprang forward; for she had sobbed. The summons had sounded; he was there; and who could sob again when he was there, and his sheltering arm warded off all grief?

She looked up at him with shining eyes, whispering:

"Do you go alone?"

A great joy blazed confidently in his eyes as he whispered in answer:

"I think I shall not go alone."

"But how, how?"

"I have two horses."

"You! You have two horses?"

"Yes, is it not riches? But we will sell them when we get to the cottage."

"To the cottage! Two horses!"

"I would I had but one for both of us."

"Yes."

"But we should not go quick enough."

"No."

He took his hand from her waist and stood away from her.

"You will not come?" he said.

"If you doubt of my coming, I will not come. Ah, do not doubt of my coming! For there is a great hoard of fears and black thoughts beating at the door, and you must not open it."

"And what can keep it shut, my Princess?"

"I think your arm, my Prince," said she; and she flew to him.

That evening King Rudolf swore that if a man were only firm enough and kept his temper (which, by the way, the King had not done, though none dared say so), he could bring any foolish girl to reason in good time. For in the softest voice, and with the strangest smile flitting to her face, the Princess Osra was pleased to bid the embassy come on the fifth day from then.

"They shall have their answer then," said she, flushing and smiling.

"It is as much as any lady could say," the Court declared; and it was reported through all Strelsau that the match was as good as made, and that Osra was to be Grand Duchess of Mittenheim.

"She's a sensible girl after all," cried Rudolf, all his anger gone.

The dream began then, before they came to the cottage. Those days she lived in its golden mists, that shut out all the cold world from her, moving through space which held but one form, and time that stood still waiting for one divine unending moment. And the embassy drew near to Strelsau.

It was night, the dead of night, and all was still in the Palace. But the sentinel by the little gate was at his post, and the gate-warden stood by the Western Gate of the city. Each was now alone, but to each, an hour ago, a man had come stealthily and silently through the darkness; and each was richer by a bag of gold than he had been before. The gold was Osra's—how should a poor student, whose whole fortune was two horses, scatter bags of gold? And other gold Osra had, aye, five hundred crowns. Would not that be a brave surprise for the poor student? And she, alone of all awake, stood looking round her room, entranced with the last aspect of it. Over the city also she looked, but in the selfishness of her joy did no more than kiss a hasty farewell to the good city folk who loved her. Once she thought that maybe, some day, he and she would steal together back to Strelsau, and sheltered by some disguise watch the King ride in splendour through the streets. But if not—why, what was Strelsau, and the people, and the rest? Ah, how long the hours were, before those two horses stood by the little gate, and the sentry and the gate-warden earned their bags of gold! So she passed the hours, the last long lingering hours.

There was a little tavern buried in the narrowest oldest street of the city. Here the poor student had lodged; here, in the back room, a man sat at a table, and two others stood before him. These two seemed gentlemen, and their air spoke of military training. They stroked long moustaches and smiled with an amusement that deference could not hide. Both were booted and wore spurs, and the man sitting at the table gave them orders.

"You will meet the embassy," he said to one, "about ten o'clock. Bring it to the place I have appointed, and wait there. Do not fail."

The officer addressed bowed and retired. A minute later his horse's hoofs clattered through the streets. Perhaps he also had a bag of gold, for the gate-warden opened the Western Gate for him, and he rode at a gallop along the river banks, till he reached the great woods that stretch to within ten miles of Strelsau.

"An hour after we are gone," said the man at the table to the other officer, "go warily, find one of the King's servants, and hand him the letter. Give no account of how you came by it, and say nothing of who you are. All that is necessary is in the letter. When you have delivered it, return here and remain in close hiding, till you hear from me again."

The second officer bowed. The man at the table rose and went out into the street. He took his way to where the Palace rose, and then skirted the wall of its gardens, till he came to the little gate. Here stood two horses, and at their heads a man.

"It is well. You may go," said the student; and he was left alone with the horses. They were good horses for a student to possess. The thought perhaps crossed their owner's mind, for he laughed softly as he looked at them. Then he also fell to thinking that the hours were long; and a fear came suddenly upon him that she would not come. It was in these last hours that doubts crept in; and he was not with her to drive them away. Would the great trial fail? Would she shrink at the last? But he would not think it of her, and he was smiling again, when the clock of the Cathedral struck two, telling him that no more than an hour now parted her from him. For she would come; the Princess would come to him, the student, led by the vision of that cottage in the dream.

Would she come? She would come; she had risen from her knees and moved to and fro in cautious silence, making her last preparations. She had written a word of love for the brother she loved—for some day, of course, Rudolf would forgive her—and she had ready all that she took with her, the five hundred crowns, one ring that she would give her lover, some clothes to serve till his loving labour furnished more. That night she had wept and she had laughed; now she neither wept nor laughed; but there was a high pride in her face and gait. She opened the door of her room, and walked down the great staircase, under the eyes of crowned Kings who hung framed upon the walls. And as she went she seemed indeed their daughter. For her head was erect, and her lips set firm in haughty dignity. Who dared to say that she did anything that a King's daughter should not do? Should not a woman love? Love should be her diadem. And so with this proud step she came through the gardens of the Palace, looking neither to right nor left, nor behind, but with her face set straight for the little gate; and she walked as she had been accustomed to walk when all Strelsau looked on her, and hailed her as its glory and its darling.

The sentry slept, or seemed to sleep. Her face was not even veiled when she opened the little gate; she would not veil her proud face, it was his to look on now when he would; and thus she stood for an instant in the gateway, while he sprang to her, and, kneeling, carried her hand to his lips.

"You are come?" he cried; for though he had believed, yet he wondered.

"I am come," she smiled. "Is not the word of a Princess sure? Ah, how could I not come?"

"See, love," said he, rising, "day dawns in royal purple for you, and golden love for me."

"The purple is for my King and the love for me," she whispered, as he led her to the horses. "Your fortune!" said she, pointing to them. "But I also have brought a dowry. Fancy, five hundred crowns!" and her mirth and happiness burst out in a laugh. It was so deliciously little, five hundred crowns!

She was mounted now and he stood by her.

"Will you turn back?" he said.

"You shall not make me angry," said she. "Come, mount."

"Aye, I must mount," said he. "For if we were found here the King would kill me."

For the first time the peril of their enterprise seemed to strike into her mind, and turned her cheek pale.

"Ah, I forgot! In my happiness I forgot. Mount, mount! Oh, if he found you!"

He mounted. Once they clasped hands; then they rode swiftly for the Western Gate.

"Veil your face," he said, and since he bade her, she obeyed, saying:

"But I can see you through the veil."

The gate stood open, and the gate-warden was not there. They were out of the city, the morning air blew cold and pure over the meadows from the river. The horses stretched into an eager willing gallop. Osra tore her veil from her face, and turned on him eyes of radiant triumph.

"It is done," she cried, "it is done."

"Yes, it is done, my Princess," said he.

"And—and it is begun, my Prince," said she.

"Yes, and it is begun," said he.

She laughed aloud in absolute joy, and for a moment he also laughed. But then his face grew grave, and he said:

"I pray you may never grieve for it."

She looked at him with eyes wide in wonder; for an instant she seemed puzzled; then she fell again to laughing.

"Grieve for it!" said she, between her merry laughs.

King Rudolf was a man who lay late in the morning, and he was not well pleased to be roused when the clock had but just struck four. Yet he sat up in his bed readily enough, for he imagined that the embassy from the Grand Duke of Mittenheim must be nearer than he thought, and, sooner than fail in any courtesy towards a Prince whose alliance he ardently desired, he was ready to submit to much inconvenience. But his astonishment was great, when, instead of any tidings from the embassy, one of his gentlemen handed him a letter, saying that a servant had received it from a stranger with instructions to carry it at once to the King; when asked if an answer were desired from his Majesty, the stranger had answered, "Not through me," and at once turned away and quickly disappeared. The King, with a peevish oath at having been roused for such a trifle broke the seal and fastenings of the letter, and opened it; and he read:

"Sire,—Your sister does not wait for the embassy, but chooses her own lover. She has met a student of the University every day for the last three weeks by the river bank." (The King started.) "This morning she has fled with him on horseback along the Western Road. If you desire a student for a brother-in-law, sleep again; if not, up and ride. Do not doubt these tidings."

There was no signature to the letter; yet the King, knowing his sister, cried:

"See whether the Princess is in the Palace. And in the meanwhile saddle my horse, and let a dozen of the Guard be at the gate."

The Princess was not in the Palace, but her women found the letter that she had left, and brought it to the King. And the King read: "Brother, whom I love best of all men in the world save one, I have left you to go with that one. You will not forgive me now, but some day forgive me. Nay, it is not I who have done it, but my love which is braver than I. He is the sweetest gentleman alive, brother, and therefore he must be my lord. Let me go, but still love me.— Osra."

"It is true," said the King; "and the embassy will be here to-day!" For a moment he seemed dazed. Yet he spoke nothing to anybody of what the letters contained, but sent word to the Queen's apartments that he went riding for pleasure. And he took his sword and his pistols; for he swore that by his own hand and by that of no other man, this "sweetest gentleman alive" should meet his death. But all, knowing that the Princess was not in the Palace, guessed that the King's sudden haste concerned her; and great wonder and speculation rose in the Palace, and presently, as the morning advanced, spread from the Palace to its environs, and from the environs to the rest of the city. For it was reported that a sentinel who had stood guard that night was missing, and that the gate-warden of the Western Gate was nowhere to be found, and that a mysterious letter had come by an unknown hand to the King, and lastly, that Princess Osra—their Princess—was gone, whether of her own will or by some bold plot of seizure and kidnapping, none knew. Thus a great stir grew in all Strelsau; men stood about the streets gossiping when they should have gone to work, while women chattered instead of sweeping their houses and dressing their children. So that when the King rode out of the courtyard of the Palace at a gallop, with twelve of the Guard behind, he could hardly make his way through the streets for the people who crowded round him, imploring him to tell them where the Princess was. When the King saw that the matter had become public, his wrath was greater still, and he swore again that the student of the University should pay the price of life for his morning ride with the Princess. And when he darted through the gate and set his horse straight along the Western Road, many of the people, neglecting all their business as folk will for excitement's sake, followed him as they best could, agog to see the thing to its end.

"The horses are weary," said the student to the Princess, "we must let them rest; we are now in the shelter of the wood."

"But my brother may pursue you," she urged, "and if he came up with you—ah, heaven forbid!"

"He will not know you have gone for another three hours," smiled he. "And here is a green bank where we can rest."

So he aided her to dismount; then, saying he would tether the horses, he led them away some distance, so that she could not see where he had posted them; and he returned to her, smiling still. Then he took from his pocket some bread, and breaking the loaf in two, gave her one half, saying:

"There is a spring just here; so we shall have a good breakfast."

"Is this your breakfast?" she asked with a wondering laugh. Then she began to eat, and cried directly: "How delicious this bread is! I would have nothing else for breakfast;" and at this the student laughed.

Yet Osra ate little of the bread she liked so well; presently she leant against her lover's shoulder, and he put his arm round her; and they sat for a little while in silence listening to the soft sounds that filled the waking woods as day grew to fulness and the sun beat warm through the sheltering foliage.

"Don't you hear the trees?" Osra whispered to her lover. "Don't you hear them? They are whispering for me what I dare not whisper."

"What is it they whisper, sweet?" he asked; he himself did no more than whisper.

"The trees whisper, 'Love, love, love.' And the wind—don't you hear the wind murmuring, 'Love, love, love'? And the birds sing, 'Love, love, love.' Aye, all the world to-day is softly whispering, 'Love, love, love.' What else should the great world whisper but my love? For my love is greater than the world." And she suddenly hid her face in her hands; and he could kiss no more than her hands, though her eyes gleamed at him from between slim white fingers.

But suddenly her hands dropped, and she leant forward as though she listened.

"What is that sound?" she asked, apprehension dawning in her eyes.

"It is but another whisper, love!" said he.

"Nay, but it sounds to me like—ah, like the noise of horses galloping."

"It is but the stream, beating over stones."

"Listen, listen, listen!" she cried springing to her feet. "They are horses' hoofs! Ah, merciful God, it is the King!" And she caught him by the hand and pulled him to his feet, looking at him with a face pale and alarmed.

"Not the King," said he. "He would not know yet. It is some one else. Hide your face, dear lady, and all will be well."

"It is the King," she cried. "Hark how they gallop on the road! It is my brother. Love, he will kill you, love, he will kill you."

"It is the King," said he, "I have been betrayed."

"The horses, the horses!" she cried. "By your love for me, the horses!"

He nodded his head, and, turning, disappeared among the trees. She stood with clasped hands, heaving breast, and fearful eyes, awaiting his return. Minutes passed and he did not come. She flung herself on her knees, beseeching heaven for his life. At last he came alone, and he bent over her, taking her hand.

"My love," said he, "the horses are gone!"

"Gone?" she cried, gripping his hand.

"Aye. This love, my love, is a wonderful thing. For I forgot to tie them, and they are gone. Yet what matter? For the King—yes, sweet, I think now it is the King—will not be here for some minutes yet, and those minutes I have still for love and life."

"He will kill you," she said.

"Yes," said he.

She looked long in his eyes; then she threw her arms about his neck, and, for the first time unasked, covered his face with kisses.

"Kiss me, kiss me," said she; and he kissed her. Then she drew back a little, but took his arm and set it round her waist. And she drew a little knife from her girdle, and showed it to him.

"If the King will not pardon us and let us love one another, I also will die," said she, and her voice was quiet and happy. "Indeed, my love, I should not grieve. Ah, do not tell me to live without you!"

"Would you obey?" he asked.

"Not in that," said she.

Thus they stood, while the sound of the hoofs drew very near. But she looked up at him and he looked at her; then she looked at the point of the little dagger, and she whispered:

"Keep your arm round me till I die."

He bent his head and kissed her once again, saying:

"My Princess, it is enough."

And she, though she did not know why he smiled, yet smiled back at him. For although life was sweet that day, yet such a death, with him, and to prove her love for him, seemed well-nigh as sweet. Thus they awaited the coming of the King.

King Rudolf and his Guards far outstripped the people who pursued them from the city, and when they came to the skirt of the wood they divided themselves into four parties, since, if they went all together, they might easily miss the fugitives whom they sought. Of these four parties one found nothing, another found the two horses, which the student himself, who had hidden them, failed to find; the third party had not gone far before they caught sight of the lovers, though the lovers did not see them; and two of them remained to watch, and if need were to intercept any attempted flight, while the other rode off to find the King and bring him where Osra and the student were, as he had commanded.

But the fourth party, with which the King was, though it did not find the fugitives, found the embassy from the Grand Duke of Mittenheim; for the ambassador, with all his train, was resting by the roadside, seeming in no haste at all to reach Strelsau. When the King suddenly rode up at great speed and came upon the embassy, an officer that stood by the ambassador—whose name was Count Sergius of Antheim—stooped down and whispered in his Excellency's ear; upon which he rose and advanced towards the King, uncovering his head and bowing profoundly; for he chose to assume that the King had ridden to meet him out of excessive graciousness and courtesy towards the Grand Duke; so that he began, to the impatient King's infinite annoyance, to make a very long and stately speech, assuring his Majesty of the great hope and joy with which his master awaited the result of the embassy; for, said he, since the King was so zealous in his cause, his master could not bring himself to doubt of success, and therefore most confidently looked to win for his bride the most exalted and lovely lady in the world, the peerless Princess Osra, the glory of the Court of Strelsau, and the brightest jewel in the crown of the King her brother. Having brought this period to a prosperous conclusion, Count Sergius took breath and began another that promised to be fully as magnificent and not a whit less long. So that, before it was well started, the King smote his hand on his thigh, and roared:

"Heavens, man, while you're making speeches, that rascal is carrying off my sister!"

Count Sergius, who was an elderly man of handsome presence and great dignity, being thus rudely and strangely interrupted, showed great astonishment and offence; but the officer by him covered his mouth with his hand to hide a smile. For the moment that the King had spoken these impetuous words he was himself overwhelmed with confusion; since the last thing that he wished the Grand Duke's ambassador to know was that the Princess, whom his master courted, had run away that morning with a student of the University of Strelsau. Accordingly he began, very hastily and with more regard for prudence than for truth, to tell Count Sergius how a noted and bold criminal had that morning swooped down on the Princess as she rode unattended outside the city and carried her off; which seemed to the ambassador a very strange story. But the King told it with great fervour, and he besought the Count to scatter his attendants all through the wood, and seek the robber; yet he charged them not to kill the man themselves but to keep him till he came. "For I have sworn to kill him with my own hand," he cried.

Now Count Sergius, however much astonished he might be, could do nothing but accede to the King's request, and he sent off all his men to scour the woods, and, mounting his horse, himself set out with them, showing great zeal in the King's service, but still thinking the King's story a very strange one. Thus the King was left alone with his two Guards and with the officer who had smiled.

"Will you not go also, sir?" asked the King.

But at this moment a man galloped up at furious speed, crying:

"We have found them, sire, we have found them!"

"Then he hasn't five minutes to live!" cried the King in fierce joy, and he lugged out his sword, adding: "The moment I set my eyes on him, I will kill him. There is no need for words between me and him."

At this speech the face of the officer grew suddenly grave and alarmed, and he put spurs to his horse and hastened after the King, who had at once dashed away in the direction in which the man had pointed; but the King had got a start and kept it, so that the officer seemed terribly frightened, and muttered to himself:

"Heaven send that he does not kill him before he knows!" And he added some very impatient words, concerning the follies of Princes, and, above all, of Princes in love.

Thus, while the ambassador and his men searched high and low for the noted robber, and the King's men hunted for the student of the University, the King, followed by two of his Guards at a distance of about fifty yards (for his horse was better than theirs), came straight to where Osra and her lover stood together; a few yards behind the Guards came the officer; and he also had by now drawn his sword.

But he rode so eagerly that he overtook and passed the King's Guards, and got within thirty yards of the King by the time that the King was within twenty of the lovers. But the King let him get no nearer, for he dug his spurs again into his horse's side, and the animal bounded forward, while the King cried furiously to his sister: "Stand away from him!"

The Princess did not heed, but stood in front of her lover (for the student was wholly unarmed), holding up the little dagger in her hand. The King laughed scornfully and angrily, thinking that Osra menaced him with the weapon, and not supposing that it was herself for whom she destined it. And, having reached them, the King leapt from his horse and ran at them, with his sword raised to strike. Osra gave a cry of terror. "Mercy!" she cried, "mercy!" But the King had no thought of mercy, and he would certainly then and there have killed her lover, had not the officer, gaining a moment's time by the King's dismounting, at this very instant come galloping up; and, there being no leisure for any explanation, he leant from his saddle as he dashed by, and, putting out his hand, snatched the King's sword away from him, just as the King was about to thrust it through his sister's lover.

But the officer's horse was going so furiously that he could not stop it for hard on forty yards; he narrowly escaped splitting his head against a great bough that hung low across the grassy path, and he dropped first his own sword and then the King's; but at last he brought his horse to a standstill, and, leaping down, ran back towards where the swords lay. But at the moment the King also ran towards them; for the fury that he had been in before was as nothing to that which now possessed him. After his sword was snatched from him he stood in speechless anger for a full minute, but then had turned to pursue the man who had dared to treat him with such insult; and now, in his desire to be at the officer, he had come very near to forgetting the student. Just as the officer came to where the King's sword lay and picked it up, the King in his turn reached the officer's sword and picked up that. The King came with a rush at the officer, who, seeing. that the King was likely to kill him, or he the King, if he stood his ground, turned tail and sped away at the top of his speed through the forest; but as he went, thinking that the time had come for plain speaking, he looked back over his shoulder and shouted:

"Sire, it's the Grand Duke himself!"

The King stopped short in sudden amazement.

"Is the man mad?" he asked. "Who is the Grand Duke?"

"It's the Grand Duke, sire, who is with the Princess. You would have killed him if I had not snatched your sword," said the officer, and he also came to a halt, but he kept a very wary eye on King Rudolf.

"I should certainly have killed him, let him be who he will," said the King. "But why do you call him the Grand Duke?"

The officer very cautiously approached the King, and, seeing that the King made no threatening motion, he at last trusted himself so close that he could speak to the King in a very low voice; and what he said seemed to astonish, please, and amuse the King immensely. For he clapped the officer on the back, laughed heartily, and cried:

"A pretty trick! on my life, a pretty trick!"

Now Osra and her lover had not heard what the officer had shouted to the King, and when Osra saw her brother returning from among the trees alone and with his sword, she still supposed that her lover must die; so she turned and flung her arms round his neck, and clung to him for a moment, kissing him. Then she faced the King, with a smile on her lips and the little dagger in her hand. But the King came up, wearing a scornful smile; and he asked her:

"What is the dagger for, my wilful sister?"

"For me, if you kill him," said she.

"You will kill yourself, then, if I kill him?"

"I would not live a moment after he was dead."

"Faith, it is wonderful!" said the King with a shrug. "Then plainly, if you cannot live without him, you must live with him. He is to be your husband, not mine. Therefore take him, if you will."

When Osra heard this, which, indeed, for joy and wonder she could hardly believe, she dropped her dagger, and, running forward, fell on her knees before her brother; catching his hand, she covered it with kisses, and her tears mingled with her kisses. But the King let her go on, and stood over her, laughing and looking at the student. Presently the student began to laugh also, and he had just advanced a step towards King Rudolf, when Count Sergius of Antheim, the Grand Duke's ambassador, came out from among the trees, riding hotly and with great zeal after the noted robber. But no sooner did the Count see the student, than he stopped his horse, leapt down with a cry of wonder, and, running up to the student, bowed very low and kissed his hand. So that when Osra looked round from her kissing of her brother's hand, she beheld the Grand Duke's ambassador kissing the hand of her lover. She sprang to her feet in wonder.

"Who are you?" she cried to the student, running in between him and the ambassador.

"Your lover and servant," said he.

"And besides?" she said.

"Why, in a month, your husband," laughed the King, taking her lover by the hand.

He clasped the King's hand, but turned at once to her, saying humbly:

"Alas, I have no cottage!"

"Who are you?" she whispered to him.

"The man for whom you were ready to die, my Princess. Is it not enough?"

"Yes, it is enough," said she; and she did not repeat her question. But the King, with a short laugh, turned on his heel, and taking Count Sergius by the arm walked off with him; and presently they called the officer and learnt fully how the Grand Duke had come to Strelsau, and how he had contrived to woo and win the Princess Osra, and finally to carry her off from the Palace.

It was an hour later when the whole of the two companies, that of the King and that of the ambassador, were all gathered together again, and had heard the story; so that when the King went to where Osra and the Grand Duke walked together among the trees, and taking each by a hand led them out, they were greeted with a great cheer; they mounted their horses, which the Grand Duke now found without any difficulty although when the need of them seemed far greater the student could not contrive to come upon them; and the whole company rode together out of the wood and along the road towards Strelsau, the King being full of jokes and hugely delighted with a trick that suited his merry fancy. But before they had ridden far they met the great crowd which had come out from Strelsau to learn what had happened to Princess Osra. And the King cried out that the Grand Duke was to marry the Princess, while his Guards, who had been with him, and the ambassador's people, spread themselves among the crowd and told the story; and when they heard it, the Strelsau folk were nearly beside themselves with amusement and delight, and thronged round Osra, kissing her hands and blessing her. The King drew back and let her and the Grand Duke ride alone together, while he followed with Count Sergius. Thus moving at a very slow pace, they came in the forenoon to Strelsau; but some one had galloped on ahead with the news, and the Cathedral bells had been set ringing, the streets were full, and the whole city given over to excitement and rejoicing. All the men were that day in love with Princess Osra, and, what is more, they told their sweethearts so; and these found no other revenge than to blow kisses and fling flowers at the Grand Duke as he rode past with Osra by his side. So they came back to the Palace, whence they had fled in the early gleams of the morning's light.

It was evening and the moon rose, fair and clear, over Strelsau. In the streets there were sounds of merriment and rejoicing; every house was bright with light; the King had sent out meat and wine for every soul in the city that none might be sad or hungry or thirsty in all the city that night; so that there was no small uproar. The King himself sat in his armchair, toasting the bride and bridegroom in company with Count Sergius of Antheim, whose dignity, somewhat wounded by the trick his master had played on him, was healing quickly under the balm of King Rudolf's graciousness. And the King said to Count Sergius:

"My lord, were you ever in love?"

"I was, sire," said the Count.

"So was I," said the King. "Was it with the Countess, my lord?"

Count Sergius's eyes twinkled demurely, but he answered:

"I take it, sire, that it must have been with the Countess."

"And I take it," said the King, "that it must have been with the Queen."

Then they both laughed; and then they both sighed; and the King, touching the Count's elbow, pointed out to the terrace of the Palace, on to which the room where they were opened. For Princess Osra and her lover were walking up and down together on this terrace. And the two shrugged their shoulders, smiling.

"With him," remarked the King, "it will have been with—"

"The Countess, sire," discreetly interrupted Count Sergius of Antheim.

"Why, yes, the Countess," said the King, and with a laugh they turned back to their wine.

But the two on the terrace also talked.

"I do not yet understand it," said Princess Osra. "For on the first day I loved you, and on the second day I loved you, and on the third and the fourth and every day I loved you. Yet the first day was not like the second, nor the second like the third, nor any day like any other.

And to-day, again, is unlike them all. Is love so various and full of changes?"

"Is it not?" he asked with a smile. "For while you were with the Queen, talking of I know not what—"

"Nor I indeed," said Osra hastily.

"I was with the King, and he, saying that forewarned was forearmed, told me very strange and pretty stories; of some a report had reached me before—"

"And yet you came to Strelsau?"

"While of others I had not heard."

"Or you would not have come to Strelsau?"

The Grand Duke, not heeding these questions, proceeded to his conclusion.

"Love, therefore," said he, "is very various. For M. de Mérosailles—"

"These are old stories," cried Osra, pretending to stop her ears.

"Loved in one way, and Stephen the smith in another, and—the Miller of Hofbau in a third."

"I think," said Osra, "that I have forgotten the Miller of Hofbau. But can one heart love in many different ways? I know that different men love differently."

"But cannot one heart love in different ways?" he smiled.

"May be," said Osra thoughtfully, "one heart can have loved." But then she suddenly looked up at him with a mischievous sparkle in her eyes. "No, no," she cried, "it was not love. It was—"

"What was it?"

"The courtiers entertained me till the King came," she said, with a blushing laugh. And looking up at him again she whispered, "Yet I am glad that you lingered for a little."

At this moment she saw the King come out on to the terrace; with him was the Bishop of Modenstein; and after the Bishop had been presented to the Grand Duke, the King began to talk with the Grand Duke, while the Bishop kissed Osra's hand and wished her joy.

"Madame," said he, "once you asked me if I could make you understand what love was. I take it you have no need for my lessons now. Your teacher has come."

"Yes, he has come." she said gently, looking at the Bishop, with friendliness. "But tell me, will he always love me?"

"Surely he will," answered the Bishop.

"And tell me," said Osra, "shall I always love him?"

"Surely," said the Bishop, again most courteously. "Yet indeed, madame," he continued, "it would seem almost enough to ask of heaven to love now and now to be loved. For the years roll on, and youth goes, and even the most incomparable beauty will yield its blossom when the season wanes; yet that sweet memory may ever be fresh and young, a thing a man can carry to his grave and raise as her best monument on his lady's tomb."

"Ah, you speak well of love," said she. "I marvel that you speak so well of love. For it is as you say; to-day in the wood it seemed to me that I had lived enough, and that even Death was but Love's servant as Life is, and both purposed solely for his better ornament."

"Men have died because they loved you, madame, and some yet live who love you," said the Bishop.

"And shall I grieve for both, my lord—or for which?"

"For neither, madame; the dead have gained peace, and they who live have escaped forgetfulness."

"But would they not be happier for forgetting?"

"I do not think so," said the Bishop, and bowing low to her again, he stood back, for he saw the King approaching with the Grand Duke; the King took him by the arm and walked on with him; but Osra's face lost the brief pensiveness that had come upon it as she talked with the Bishop, and turning to her lover, she stretched out her hands to him, saying:

"I wish there was a cottage, and that you worked for bread, while I made ready for you at the cottage, and then ran far, far, far down the road to watch and wait for your coming."

"Since a cottage was not too small, a palace will not be too large," said he, catching her in his arms.

Thus the heart of Princess Osra found its haven and its rest; for a month later she was married to the Grand Duke of Mittenheim in the Cathedral of Strelsau, having utterly refused to take any other place for her wedding. Again she and he rode forth together through the Western Gate; and the King rode with them on their way till they came to the woods. Here he paused and all the crowd that accompanied him stopped also; and they all waited till the sombre depths of the glades hid Osra and her lover from their sight. Then, leaving them thus riding together to their happiness, the people returned home, sad for the loss of their darling Princess. But for consolation, and that their minds might the less feel her absence, they had her name often on their lips; and the poets and storytellers composed many stories about her, not grounded on fact, as are those which have been here set forth, but the fabric of idle imaginings, wrought to please the fancy of lovers or to wake the memories of older folk. So that, if a stranger goes now to Strelsau, he may be pardoned if it seem to him that all mankind was in love with Princess Osra. Nay, and those stories so pass all fair bounds that if you listen to them, you will come near to believing that the Princess also had found some love for all the men who had given her their love. Thus to many she is less a woman who once lived and breathed, than some sweet image under whose name they fondly group all the virtues and the charms of her whom they love best, each man fashioning for himself from his own chosen model her whom he calls his Princess. Yet it may be that for some of them who so truly loved her, her heart had a moment's tenderness. Who shall tell all the short-lived dreams that come and go, the promptings and stirrings of a vagrant inclination? And who would pry too closely into these secret matters? May we not more properly give thanks to heaven that the thing is as it is? For surely it makes greatly for the increase of joy and entertainment in the world, and of courtesy and true tenderness, that the heart of Princess Osra—or of what lady you may choose, sir, to call by her name—should flutter in pretty hesitation here and there and to and fro a little, before it flies on a straight wing to its destined and desired home. And if you be not the Prince for your Princess, why, Sir, your case is a sad one. Yet there have been many such, and still there is laughter as well as tears in the tune to which the world spins round:—

> But still a Ruby kindles in the Vine,
> And many a Garden by the Water blows.

Wear your willow then, as the Marquis de Mérosailles wore his, lightly and yet most courteously; or like the Bishop of Modenstein (for so some say), with courage and self-mastery. That is, if wear it you must. You remember what the Miller of Hofbau thought?